Lucy Did The Only Possible Thing She Could Think Of. She Reached Up To Tangle Her Fingers In Ethan's Thick Hair And Pulled His Head Down To Hers

She felt his hand, still around her waist, spread and lift, and next thing she was on tiptoe, planted against the length of him like ivy. He held back slightly, his brow still furrowed in a frown.

She tugged him closer and he sank into her mouth. Hot and humid, his tongue felt satiny slick, dancing with hers. She fought to breathe. He was so strong. His arms crushed her to him. The tension in his neck, each and every finger spread wide on her back, the muscles in his thighs pressed up against hers—it was all leashed power.

Her mind shut down. Her blood was roaring. She wanted him unleashed.

Dear Reader,

Celebrate the conclusion of 2005 with the six fabulous novels available this month from Silhouette Desire. You won't be able to put down the scintillating finale to DYNASTIES: THE ASHTONS once you start reading Barbara McCauley's *Name Your Price.* He believes she was bought off by his father…she can't fathom his lack of trust. Neither can deny the passion still pulsing between them.

We are so excited to have Caroline Cross back writing for Desire…and with a brand-new miniseries, MEN OF STEELE. In *Trust Me,* reunited lovers have more to deal with than just relationship troubles—they are running for their lives. Kristi Gold kicks one out of the corral as she wraps up TEXAS CATTLEMAN'S CLUB: THE SECRET DIARY with her story of secrets and scandals, *A Most Shocking Revelation.*

Enjoy the holiday cheer found in Joan Elliott Pickart's *A Bride by Christmas,* the story of a wedding planner who believes she's jinxed never to be a bride herself. Anna DePalo is back with another millionaire playboy who finally meets his match, in *Tycoon Takes Revenge.* And finally, welcome brand-new author Jan Colley to the Desire lineup with *Trophy Wives,* a story of lies and seduction not to be missed.

Be sure to come back next month when we launch a new and fantastic twelve-book family dynasty, THE ELLIOTTS.

Melissa Jeglinski

Melissa Jeglinski
Senior Editor
Silhouette Books

Please address questions and book requests to:
Silhouette Reader Service
U.S.: 3010 Walden Ave., P.O. Box 1325, Buffalo, NY 14269
Canadian: P.O. Box 609, Fort Erie, Ont. L2A 5X3

TROPHY
WIVES
Jan Colley

Published by Silhouette Books

America's Publisher of Contemporary Romance

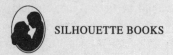 **SILHOUETTE BOOKS**

ISBN 0-373-76698-X

TROPHY WIVES

Copyright © 2005 by Janet Colley

This edition published by arrangement with Harlequin Books S.A.

Visit Silhouette Books at www.eHarlequin.com

Printed in U.S.A.

JAN COLLEY

lives in Christchurch, New Zealand, with her long-suffering fireman and two cats who don't appear to suffer much at all. She started writing after selling a business because at tender middle age, she is a firm believer in spending her time doing something she loves. A member of the Romance Writers of New Zealand and Romance Writers of Australia, she is determined that this book will be the first of many. She enjoys reading, traveling and watching rugby, and would be tickled pink to hear from readers. E-mail her at vagabond23@yahoo.com.

Thanks for the support of romance writing organizations everywhere, and all the multipublished authors who give up their time to help the newbies.

One

Her heels clicked across the big expanse of floor, quick and sharp. Head swiveling, she dismissed the individuals milling this way and that. Where *was* he?

Who could blame him for not waiting? She was nearly an hour late, after all. Could she never get anything right?

There. Sitting alone by the domestic arrivals gate. Exactly where he was supposed to be.

Lucy replaced her impatient expression with a determined smile. Ethan Rae. Mr. Ethan Rae. She started quickly toward him across the concourse of the small airport, mentally chanting an apology. Mr. Rae. I am so sorry.

Her heels made a cheerful ditty on the polished linoleum. The sound kept up with her, and, as she drew level with the slumped figure in the chair, she was astonished to see no movement.

He was asleep!

Hot guilt washed over her and she nervously chewed her bottom lip. She was in *so* much trouble. Tom had already scalped her for the mix-up over ordering the luxury van that they used to escort clients from the airport to the lodge. By the time she had worked it out, it was too late to do anything else but collect him herself.

"Wha-a-a-t?" her half brother had practically yelled down the phone. "You can't pick him up in the Beast. Couldn't you have ordered him a car—limo, rental—anything?"

"Everything is booked. There's an APEC conference on in town, remember?"

"What about your car?"

She grimaced. "I'm having it cleaned. Why didn't you check his arrival time, Tom? We had a deal."

"Well, yes," he conceded, and Lucy was gratified to hear some guilt in his voice. "I've got rather a lot on my plate at the moment." His heavy sigh down the line was timed for maximum sympathy.

"You're not the only one. Besides you know how I am. You're supposed to check these things." Lucy tried to recall the fax containing details of the man's booking. "Who ever uses the twenty-four-hour clock, anyway?"

Tom sighed again. "Well, get here as soon as you can. And apologize like hell. Drinks start at seven-thirty. I need you here."

The current object of her agitation snoozed on, oblivious. She felt a headache twinge behind her eyes. She stood, clutching her wallet with both hands in front of her, wondering how to proceed.

Good suit, she noted, being rather an expert at clothes. Conservative, but expensive. The jacket was unfastened, revealing a stone-colored shirt wrapped around a long, lean torso with impressively broad shoulders. Long legs, crossed at the ankles, thrust into soft leather shoes. Well-tended hands lay on the armrests of the narrow chair, fingers splayed, giving the impression that he was ready to spring into action in an instant.

The thick hair on his bowed head was the color of bitter chocolate, with a fine tracing of silver at the neatly trimmed sideburns. It would grow wavy, she decided, if it were allowed. His skin was tan and smooth with a dark bluish shadow around his relaxed jaw.

She guessed he was little more than thirty, younger than she'd expected. Only the very rich could afford to stay at Summerhill, her family homestead, and enjoy the exclusive hunting, trekking and charters they offered. Usually the very rich were older—and accompanied.

A warm shiver of interest stirred, deep inside. Maybe her day was about to get better, after all.

The man's eyelids stirred. Lucy drew herself up to her full five-foot-five, inhaling apprehensively. Apology time. Her mind clicked into her best customer-service mode, her face into a smile she hoped conveyed apology and courtesy. She cleared her throat gently. "Mr. Rae? Ethan Rae?"

She watched his eyes squeeze tight. His mouth twisted in a grimace, then softened. The fingers of his left hand flexed then curled around the arm of his chair. When she looked back at his face, his eyelids had risen, but, because of his slumped position, he was looking down at her feet. Lucy waited.

And waited. He appeared to be conducting a fairly thorough examination of her painted toenails, her feet encased in strappy turquoise sandals, then her legs and finally the hem of the sea-green tunic that floated below the waist of her silk pants. He was actually studying her—minutely. Not even bothering to grant her the courtesy and respect of looking at her face.

Lucy shifted slightly, and the breath that escaped from her lips had no taint of apology now.

But still he dawdled, his shuttered eyes resting now on her hips, a tiny line creasing his forehead. And then they traveled on, up over the swell of her breasts. Instinctively, she tugged the edge of her blue-green silk shawl a little higher as his eyes lingered over pale skin exposed by the spaghetti straps of her tunic.

By the time his gaze reached her face, she felt as flushed as a schoolgirl. But it wasn't schoolgirl indignation she was feeling. Discomfort jostled with appreciation of his dark good looks, and a little thrill of awareness that she wasn't the only one pleasantly surprised by the meeting. A knowing and rather pleased smile quirked her brows as she met his gaze.

Not that she cared, but no sign of apology crossed his unwavering look. Pale blue eyes, in shocking contrast to his deeply tanned face, met hers and continued to scrutinize bluntly, curiously, in a haze of drowsy appreciation.

Lucy lifted her chin. "Mr. Ethan Rae?" She was thankful that there was no hint in her voice of the butterflies that leapt to life in her midriff.

Still regarding her intently, his head inclined an inch. Lucy exhaled. "Lucy McKinlay." She offered her hand. "I've come to drive you out to Summerhill."

He blinked, ignoring her outstretched hand, and slowly raised himself to his feet. She stepped back involuntarily. His long lean frame unwound itself to loom above her, with only inches between them.

Her heart gave a lazy, rolling thump, just once.

Ethan Rae stretched and ran one hand through his hair. An interesting little cowlick flicked up at the front, incongruous when matched with his stern and conservative air. She rather liked it.

His eyes narrowed, crinkling at the corners and pierced her with a glittering lance. "Evening." His voice was deep, lazy.

Lucy pursed her lips to stop the teasing smile that threatened to erupt. This man was a client. Flirting would be unprofessional and inappropriate.

But tempting. Very tempting… "I'm sorry I'm late, Mr. Rae."

He glanced at the silver timepiece on his wrist. "One hour late."

Three short words, but Lucy lost herself in the deep, flowing timbre of his voice. "Sorry," she said again, too distracted to look contrite. "Do you have luggage?"

His pale orbs flicked to an expensive-looking bag under the chair beside his.

Lucy reached for the bag. "You travel light."

Ethan Rae intercepted her with his shoulder, all signs of drowsiness gone, and hoisted the bag. "I've got it."

Lucy turned and led him through the terminal toward the exit, totally aware of his presence behind her, of his eyes on her. She consciously tightened every inch of her spine, lifted her head and walked as if she were on a catwalk. The shawl dipped down at the back and she did nothing to halt the slide. She didn't mind at all showing off the almost backless tunic top, loving how the silk swished and rustled with the movement of her thighs. If he wanted to look, he could look. It might take his mind off her tardiness.

He was the most attractive man her eyes had been treated to in a long while. She obviously spent too much time with older men.

"Did you have a hard night?" she asked brightly, determined to charm him. It was a seventy-minute drive to their destination. Lust was uncomfortable enough. Disapproving silence would be worse.

Ethan blinked as the crisp night air touched his face. He drew level with her in long gliding strides. His brows rose at her question but he did not speak.

A man of few words, she deduced. "You were sleeping."

"Long flight," was his eventual response, matched with a lengthy gaze.

A man who considers every word uttered to him and by him. The commentary hummed in her brain. "From Sydney?"

He nodded briefly. "Started a couple of days ago. From Saudi."

Lucy nodded and turned to the pay-to-go station, feeding her ticket and some coins into the slot to pay for parking. Then she faced him and took a deep breath. "About the transportation…" She reluctantly gestured toward the filthiest and most ancient four-wheel-drive in the park. "I have to apologize. Again."

Ethan stopped and stared disbelievingly. She swung herself up into the driver's seat of the Land Rover and leaned over to unlock and push open his door. After a few seconds of hesitation, his hand snaked around the passenger door to pull up the lock on the back. Lucy heard the slide of his bag in the back while she gave the passenger seat a quick and ineffectual swipe. Grimacing, nose twitching, he eased himself in beside her and settled back.

She put the key in the ignition and then turned to face him. "You see, I was supposed to order you a car. But I got the times mixed up."

"Yours?" he asked, staring at the dust-covered dash, the mud and plant matter under his expensive shoes, the barely transparent windscreen. Preparing to rest his arm along the doorframe, he thought better of it and leaned forward to stare at a dubious dark stain running along the bottom of the window.

"No. Mine is—indisposed at the moment," Lucy told him, backing out of the parking space. "Mrs. Seymour's horrible little bichon frise indisposed it this afternoon." Her mouth turned down as she recalled the whining woman from Auckland and her grotty little dog, whom she had gratefully delivered to the airport just a few hours ago. When she glanced at him his brows were raised in query. "Put it this way," she told him with a wry smile. "You think this smells bad…"

The Land Rover shuddered to a halt before the arm of the exit station. "By the time I found out about the car mix-up, it was too late to find any other vehicle. Normally, I wouldn't dream of picking up a client in the Beast."

Lucy laboriously wound the window down, then entered the ticket into the slot and watched the barrier arm rock and bounce up. The vehicle lurched forward unsteadily while she rewound the stubborn window. She could feel his gaze on her but kept her eyes on the road ahead.

"You pick up all your guests looking like that?" His tone had lost the sleepy, lazy quality of before.

"We're having cocktails tonight in honor of a VIP. The other guests are welcome to attend. It's sort of a meet-and-greet thing." She shot him a welcoming look. "If you're not too tired."

His eyes flashed over her. "Wide awake, suddenly," he told her enigmatically.

Lucy felt her face flame in a burst of pleasure and focused on the road. It was nice to be noticed, especially after the day she'd had. A million errands, the loathsome dog and her error over Ethan's ETA meant she'd only had time for the quickest of showers and a lick of makeup to go with the cocktail outfit that was supposed to impress tonight.

"McKinlay," he said, dragging his seatbelt over his shoulder. "You're part of the Summerhill family."

Lucy nodded.

"What's your role in the operation?"

"I run errands. Pick-ups, drop-offs. And I look after the wives and partners of the guests."

Ethan squinted at her, nodding slowly. "You look after the trophy wives of the trophy hunters." It wasn't a question.

Lucy was surprised at the disdain in his voice. "We don't put it quite like that," she said carefully.

"No? What would you call a woman who is married— or not—to someone thirty years older and loaded?"

"Lucky?" Lucy quipped, but judging from the compression of his mouth, he didn't appreciate her joke.

She'd have to tread carefully during the next few days and restrain her occasionally irreverent perspective. The VIP they were wining tonight was Magnus Anderson, the founder of the exclusive club that Summerhill was part of. There were fewer than twenty-five lodges worldwide recommended by the club's bi-annual publication, the revered Global List.

Magnus and his wife had landed yesterday. They were supposedly here for a week's delayed honeymoon, but their guest had indicated his displeasure at certain rumors regarding the quality and financial stability of the Summerhill operation. Lucy would do or say nothing to jeopardize their place in the organization.

If Summerhill were ousted from the club, there was nowhere to go but down.

"What does entertaining the wives involve?"

Again, Lucy pondered. "Whatever they want to do to stop them from getting bored and lonely and intruding on their husbands' hunting. I can provide information, or an itinerary. Transport." She saw his eyes flick around the filthy cab. "Make bookings. Or I can escort them places."

One of his dark brows arched curiously.

Lucy shrugged. "Shopping. Bungee-jumping. Lunch. Whatever…"

Ethan frowned out the windscreen. She got the distinct impression that she and her clients had just gone down a notch in his estimation. But an instant later she felt his raking gaze again. "Like a professional companion."

"I suppose I am." She smiled brightly and nodded. "Some like company, but sometimes they just want bookings made or suggestions."

"Enjoy it?" he asked, rather tersely.

Lucy nodded. "Most of the time."

He was silent as the big motor swept a roundabout and eased into the light flow of traffic. Several minutes passed until she hit the city limits and headed toward the west coast. Dusk had done its worst and the city lights behind cast a softly mauve glow.

Ethan stretched back in his seat and yawned widely.

"Sleep if you want," she offered. "It's over an hour's drive."

He rubbed his hands together and leaned forward to

peer at the instrument panel. "Colder than I expected. I left forty degrees."

"What were you doing in the Middle East?"

"Developing a tourist resort." He fiddled with the heating dial. "Winter in New Zealand should be a refreshing change."

Suddenly a cloud of chaff puffed out from the vents. Her breath caught in her throat as she watched the millions of particles rise up to the cab's ceiling and then settle, painfully slowly, onto his expensively clad knees.

Lucy bit her bottom lip and forbade herself to smile. When she dared glance at him again, he was shaking his head.

"Dare you to laugh," he murmured, but his mouth had pursed into a reluctant grin.

Now that was worth waiting for. She allowed her own smile to form. The glint in his pale eyes and a flash of white teeth lit up his face, revealing the leanness of his cheeks and no-nonsense jawline, the straight length of his nose, and his lips—not full but not ungenerous either.

At least there was a semblance of humor there. The situation wasn't hopeless. "I wouldn't dream of it," she told him, rolling her eyes. "Sorry."

His wry grunt reassured her. "I know little about Summerhill," he commented. "It used to be a high-country station, didn't it?"

Lucy automatically recited a brief history of her heritage. "The house was built in the late 1860s by a wealthy Scotsman who farmed, at that time, about one hundred thousand acres. Over the years, parts of the land were sold off—to other farmers, to the conservation department. The original family sold the remaining forty thousand acres to my grandfather."

She paused as the familiar ache settled over her heart. Her own father had continued to farm in the very toughest high-country conditions to provide for his young family. Until her mother had left when Lucy was eight.

"Only about half of it is arable. The rest is…" she broke off, a lump in her throat. How to describe it? Unbearably beautiful? Savage and remote? Her own special kingdom? "Mountains, forest, a gorge…" Pride and regret swelled the lump in her throat, rendering her voice uncharacteristically thready. Her heritage had long suffered her indifference. And now, when its importance to her transcended everything else, it might be dangerously late and dependent on others.

She felt Ethan's interested gaze and shook her head, knowing whatever words she chose would be inadequate. "Well, it's something. Wild and remote."

She ventured a glance. He nodded as if he understood.

"My half brother, Tom, changed the dynamics of the farm about five years ago to incorporate luxury accommodation and a restaurant, and he set up mountain hunting safaris, trekking and adventure tours."

What she didn't say was that Tom had set up the lodge against their father's wishes. But her father had no fight left in him and Lucy was off overseas, enjoying herself.

"Who are your main clients?"

"Americans. Germans. Indonesians. And you Australians."

"What sort of adventure tours?"

"Jet-boating. White-water rafting is popular. Heliskiing. Fishing—the Rakaia River that flows through the farm is famous for salmon. Have you been to the South Island before?"

He shook his head. "My mother owns a small kiwifruit holding in North Island. I try to get over once or twice a year."

"It's quite different," Lucy explained. "North Island farms seem so…civilized in comparison."

"What do you farm?"

"Beef." She'd do well to change the subject. The farm wasn't high on Tom's list of priorities at the moment. And Tom's priorities were a mystery to all. "Are you warm enough?"

As if she'd reminded him, he grunted and absently brushed at the debris on his trousers.

"How long is your holiday?" she ventured.

He stifled a yawn and shrugged. "Undecided. Few days, maybe a week." He faced her and she felt his gaze move over her like a slow burn. "Problem?"

"No. We're not too busy at the moment." If we get kicked out of the club, she thought, business will slow permanently.

"Perhaps I'll make use of your escort service."

"Pardon?"

"Just think of me as a trophy wife."

She laughed. "I think that might be a bit difficult."

"Why's that, Ms. McKinlay?" he asked in that wonderful baritone that washed over her skin like a caress.

Lucy kept her eyes on the road, but her lips tightened at the effect his deep gravelly voice, slow and so masculine, had on her nerve endings. Calm down, Flirty Luce; he's out of bounds… "Why don't you call me Lucy?" Ethan only nodded and she felt a girlish kick of pleasure at the knowledge that he would be staying and might be needing company.

"Who lives at Summerhill?"

"My half brother, Tom. And Ellie, the housekeeper. She's been with us forever." Lucy's voice softened fondly. "She was Dad's primary caregiver when he had the stroke." She glanced at Ethan. "My father died three months ago."

"Sorry to hear that," he murmured.

You wouldn't be if you had seen him, Lucy thought. Dying was preferable to living the way Thomas McKinlay Senior had lived those last few months after the stroke. He'd been totally incapacitated: unable to walk, talk, feed or bathe himself. She couldn't bear it....

"And you?"

Ethan's question startled her. "What?"

"Do you live at Summerhill?"

"A lot of the time. I have an apartment in town. It's handy if I have late pick-ups or drop-offs."

"You look like a city girl."

Lucy laughed. "I can't decide if that's a compliment or not. What does a city girl look like?"

He took his time answering. "Too delicate to be a farm girl, I suppose."

"Delicate? Looks can be deceiving. I delivered my fair share of lambs and calves as a kid. And I like to ride. Do you? We have horses."

Ethan nodded and, undeterred by his earlier experience, he reached his hand out to the instrument panel again. "Haven't ridden in years. I'd like that."

Techno music blared out from the ancient radio. The alacrity with which the volume was turned down prompted a smile from Lucy. "I bet you're a jazz man."

Another flash of white teeth. "Now, how would that be obvious?"

Oh, I dunno. The slow stroke of your fingers over your jaw. The black-velvet voice. And eyes that should, by rights, freeze hell over, but instead crackle with heat. Aloud, she told him she had once caught the New Orleans Mardi Gras, and they discovered they had actually been there the same year.

The conversation progressed onto a range of artists. Ethan was obviously an aficionado, whereas Lucy had a wide range of tastes and wouldn't be pinned down to specifics.

She smiled into the night. It was fun to pass the miles in good-natured banter. The next few days promised to be interesting.

But Ethan took issue when Lucy lamented that she could not dance to jazz. "There's dancing, and there's dancing," he told her, and the warmth inside the car seemed to wind up a notch. "Jazz is sultry. Music for hot nights." He paused, then took a soft hissing breath. "Or cold nights and a big fire."

His voice sizzled along the back of her neck. Lucy imagined that voice spilling into her ear millimeters away, pressed up close in the light of a leaping fire.

Her throat went dry. "Are you warm enough?" she asked, forgetting she had already inquired.

"Plenty."

They passed the last half hour in silence. He hunkered back in his seat with his head on the rest and appeared to drift off to sleep. There was little traffic and the silence wasn't at all awkward. Lucy had learned these last six months to read people well and act accordingly. There were times to fill every second with conversation, and times to sit and let the other person take the lead. She could be quiet, if that's what the client wanted. Funny, when she remembered always being in trouble at school for excessive chatter. Always being in trouble at school for everything….

She glanced often at the man at her side. He was as delicious as a Chocolate Thin biscuit, she decided, then changed her mind with a grin. Lean, not thin, shoulders *that* broad, or legs—as far as she could decently tell—that looked long, strong and robust could never be termed thin. No way, no how.

So far, she liked everything about him. He had an honest, appreciative way of looking at her. He digested every word spoken to him and considered every word he spoke back. It showed in the long pauses punctuating his conversation, as if he were listening intently for the truth in your voice.

His voice: lazy, deep and gritty. Slow, almost a drawl. John Wayne! Lucy almost gasped when she realized he sounded just like the cowboy in the movies. "A man's gotta *do* what a man's gotta do...."

Altogether an intriguing package. She wondered what his marital status was. He wore no ring, but that meant little.

She turned off at the sign to the nearby ski village and began the gentle incline, flashing through the tiny settlements that nestled beside the Rakaia River in the shadow of the Southern Alps. With nothing but the drone of the engine in her ears, it seemed she was the only person awake in the world.

Finally they turned into a long driveway. Lucy checked her watch. Seven-twenty. The cattle stop at the start of the gravel drive caused Ethan to stir and rub his face briskly.

The house made a picture. Against a black canvas, the rambling two-story structure glittered impressively from every room. Summerhill was a kilometer from the road and flanked by the Rakaia River, about three hundred metres away, with sturdy foothills to the back. Slender poplars lined the driveway and marched on to meet the willows Lucy's grandfather had planted alongside the river.

Lucy pulled to one side, turned the ignition off, and they stepped out into the cool night air. Ethan stretched and retrieved his bag from the back.

"I'll show you to your room."

He followed her up the steps to the entrance. She stopped at the top and gestured for him to precede her into the house.

They stepped into the wide entrance, a massive area itself, yet dominated by a huge stairway. An imposing wapiti stag head with fourteen-point antlers stared balefully at an early twenties portrait of the house on the opposite wall. The old Oriental rug under their feet was faded now, but with enough color to give the kauri wood of the paneling and floorboards a lift.

The hallway was deserted.

"Follow me, Mr. Rae."

"Ethan," he murmured, looking around, seemingly in no hurry. He followed her up the staircase, head swiveling as she pointed out where to find the dining room and bar, the covered swimming pool and other outside amenities.

She stopped by a closed door with a key in the lock and pushed her way into a large and sumptuously decorated room. She noted with satisfaction that the rich velvet drapes were closed and the gas fire, housed in the best of all the antique fireplaces in the lodge, glowed cozily. Moving to the huge bed, she flicked the bedside lamps on.

It was a handsome room with great views through the floor-to-ceiling double doors out to the balcony. A little masculine for her taste—but comfortable, with two sofas to relax on, a good sized desk, table and chairs and an adjoining bathroom with shower and spa-bath.

Ethan tossed his bag onto the bed and made a quick

inspection of the facilities then came to stand right in front of her. "Looks comfortable." He nodded approvingly.

She offered him the key and began to turn away, but then hesitated. "Please do join us for drinks, if you're not too tired. The trophy room is left at the bottom of the stairs. If not, call room service and they can send up anything you wish."

He inclined his head. "Thanks. I'll freshen up, see how I feel."

Lucy stared up into eyes that could melt the coldest heart. How could ice-blue eyes be so warm? A buzz of sensual awareness lifted the hairs on the back of her neck.

Cause and effect. Bemused, she felt her belly clench and the skin of her exposed cleavage prickle. Knowing full well what that signaled, she took a quick step back, drawing the folds of cool silk closer. A raging red flush clawing up her chest and throat would look fetching in the glow of the fire. Not.

She nodded and turned on her heel. A small smile curved her lips as she sashayed down the hallway. Of course he would come down for drinks. He *had* to.

He made her feel reckless. He made her want to flirt. But then, she had always been flighty. Everyone said so.

Two

Ethan expelled a lengthy breath as the door closed behind her. Her fresh scent still clung to his nostrils, but the rustle of the fabric of that stunning outfit was gone.

Blindsided, he thought, stroking his chin and staring at the closed door. Like a skier in an avalanche, right from that first long look.

He was horny, that was all. It had been way too long since his last break, and the Middle East wasn't the easiest place to spend a year.

Shrugging out of his jacket, he scooped up his toilet bag, walked into the bathroom and turned the shower on. He scrubbed away his traveling grime and jet lag, but couldn't quite get the sight of her from his mind's eye or the zing of berries and roses from his nostrils.

Ethereal was the word that sprang to mind. All that milky skin from her face, down her throat and over the top of her shoulders. Even her beautifully shaped lips were pale. Only her eyes, a warm Mediterranean blue, made her real. Otherwise, he could well believe her to be a fairy princess in a story somewhere, dappled sunlight on her gossamer threads.

Ethan turned the shower off, chuckling at his cheesy notions.

But her eyes held secrets and laughter and womanly desires. She was not indifferent to him, and she was too young to be subtle about it. Not that he minded forward women. She wanted him, all right. He bet she was even now thinking about him, his dark hands on her white skin, his mouth crushed to hers… Get a grip!

Too young, too innocent and light years away from the women he generally dated. He tied a towel around his midriff and padded back into the bedroom. Not to mention probably a gold digger. Women who worked in an environment of money usually wanted it for themselves.

Women and money. As he dressed, a tiny part of him admired the single-minded way young and beautiful women went after money. They smelled it. They coveted it. They would do anything to get it. Which reminded him. That was part of the reason he was here.

He retrieved his phone from the suit jacket he'd tossed on the bed and stabbed numbers into it.

Magnus was more of a father to him than his own. An honorable man. A sensible man. A widower for many years, it didn't surprise Ethan he wanted company again, someone to contemplate retirement with.

But to marry a woman thirty years his junior having known her barely two months was totally out of character. When Ethan, just days ago, had received an anonymously sent packet of newspaper clippings regarding the death of a multimillionaire Texan, he could not ignore it.

The phone was answered on the third ring. He recognized the casual voice of the man he'd met briefly the day before in Sydney. As they spoke, Ethan sat on the bed, phone cradled between his ear and shoulder, and reached for his briefcase. He tipped the clippings out onto the bed. The top one showed Magnus and the new Mrs. Anderson on their wedding day.

"I've started with her background," the private investigator told him. "Julie May Stratton. Born in West Virginia, in the mountains. Father was a trapper. Six kids."

While the man spoke, Ethan sifted through some of the other clippings. They were the worst kind of scandal sheets. Grainy and dated photos, outrageous headlines. Hillbilly Makes Good, one screamed. The Millionaire and the Trapper's Daughter! said another.

He listened to her early history, up until she was working as an air hostess. Ethan bent down and shoved his feet into shoes.

"She finished up in Dallas. And that's where she met her husband. Twenty years older son from his first marriage, and from good ranching stock. His family wasn't happy. Hell, the whole city wasn't happy. Linc Sherman the Third was one of the most eligible divorced men in Dallas."

Ethan listened to the sound of papers being rustled.

"When he died, the city's press and broadcasters really did a number on Julie. For months, she was practically under house arrest, with the family ranting and raving."

Ethan smiled. "You sound almost sympathetic."

"Call me old-fashioned, Mr. Rae, but I like a bit of evidence. They were alone on the yacht. No firearms on board that had been fired. No residue on her. She claims to have had one too many glasses of champagne and didn't even hear him get up. It was all very convenient, but also very circumstantial."

No Charges Brought! headed one of the most vitriolic of the clippings. The article went on to lament the intelligence of the entire Dallas police force. Ethan's mouth tightened in distaste. The press was all for implementing the death penalty in this particular case.

The investigator told him of the political pressure the police were under because of Linc Sherman's standing in the city. But forensics, medical experts, lie detectors—she came through them all. And a witness had seen a yacht close to where the Shermans were moored. It was identical to one Julie had told police she'd seen earlier that evening, one her husband had waved to but gotten no response. Despite massive publicity all over the States, no one had come forward to be eliminated from the inquiry as a suspect and the yacht was never found.

After the Dallas police had wound up their investigation, Julie Stratton Sherman had moved to Australia, changed her name to Juliette and shaved four years off her age. Hardly incriminating, but still…

"What was he worth?" He whistled at the answer. "Big step up for a hillbilly."

Even after paying off a hit man, Ethan reasoned, it would be a huge inheritance. But then, she hadn't gotten anything yet. Why would she be in a hurry to kill off another husband? Forty million dollars wouldn't be much good to her if she were in jail serving time for murder.

His tension eased a little. His shoelaces tied, he sat back and retrieved the phone from his shoulder. "Keep digging. I want to know every move she's made since she's been in Australia. Every place she's lived, every party she's been to, every boyfriend she's had."

Ethan broke the connection, stood and moved to his open briefcase on the desk. Until the private investigator reported back to him with something more concrete than innuendo, he planned to keep a very close eye on the new Mrs. Anderson.

He checked his watch. Barely twenty minutes had passed since Lucy had shown him to his room. He lifted out the report he had compiled on the Middle Eastern project. He wanted everything relevant at his fingertips in the morning. Preparation was key and his boss demanded the best.

Juliette Anderson and the completed development were not the only pressing matters on his agenda. His hand rested briefly on another file and he felt the familiar zip of excitement tickle his shoulder blades. Turtle Island. Possibly his greatest triumph. If he could pull this sale off, it would be the deal of the century.

It would also have just that small whiff of revenge about it....

He checked his appearance in the mirror and pocketed the key Lucy had given him. You made a plan and you stuck to it, he thought as he left the room. That was the only way to get ahead. Nothing left to chance. Not like his father.

The remembered taste of poverty slicked over his tongue like diesel. It was a taste you never forgot. That taste had spurred Ethan to put his own goals in motion at an early age to ensure his comfort and security. He had spent fifteen years working his way up in Magnus's corporation. Now he was at the very top, on the verge of the biggest and most satisfying deal of his career. Then he would have the freedom to decide what the next fifteen years would bring.

Not too bad for trailer trash.

He found his way to the trophy room bar. Plaque-mounted stags' heads and plump fish, not surprisingly, adorned the walls. There was a hunters' gallery in an alcove, and upholstered window seats all around, jazzed up with bright cushions. One wall was entirely glass and he'd bet there was a great view in the daytime.

A heavily jowled man behind the bar was handing an Asian couple some well-dressed glasses. Ethan glanced around and spotted Lucy over by a huge stone fireplace. She and Magnus looked up as he approached.

"Ethan, my boy," his boss boomed, with a broad smile and a hefty clap on the back.

Ethan answered his smile with one of his own. In the six months since he'd last seen Magnus, he appeared to have lost weight and shed a few wrinkles. Ethan thought he'd never looked better. They shook hands warmly, then Magnus tugged him forward and turned to bring his wife into the fray.

Juliette Anderson was a stunner. Statuesque, golden, gracious. She looked like a beauty queen, vibrantly apart from and above other mere mortals. Glossier hair, brighter eyes, skin that glowed. Surely that flawless complexion, swept-up hair and perfectly buffed fingernails could only be achieved with a large team of stylists on hand around the clock.

"Ethan, it gives me great pleasure to introduce my wife. Juliette, meet Ethan Rae, a man I consider as close as a son."

Magnus stepped back, releasing Ethan's hand.

"Pleasure, Ms. Anderson," Ethan murmured.

"Please, Juliette."

He saw Lucy offer Magnus something off the heavy platter of hors d'oeuvres she carried. Narrowing his gaze, he murmured "Julie," in a lowered voice.

Her golden eyes opened wide, then a definite arctic blast seemed to wash across her face. She took his hand. "Ju. Lee. Ette." Her voice also lowered and there was a peculiarly intense diction to the syllables.

"Juliette," Ethan repeated smoothly.

The woman nodded tightly. Lucy intervened with her platter of nibbles. When he glanced back at Juliette, her face had reverted to serene loveliness.

Ethan believed in laying his cards on the table. As soon as he could get her on her own, he would find out just what her game was. At least now, she knew he was watching her.

"Good evening," came a voice from behind him. "Can I get you something from the bar?"

"My brother Tom," Lucy told him.

"Half brother," Tom corrected, extending his hand.

Ethan took an immediate and unexpected dislike to the man. Was it the heavy, untoned look of him? The moist softness of his hand? Or the almost imperceptible glance of disdain that he shot at Lucy while correcting her? Ethan wasn't usually so quick to judge, but he trusted his instincts. "Wine. White and dry, thanks."

The man turned away. Ethan watched him walk up to the bar, thinking there was little familial resemblance. Lucy was delicate, with a purity of proportion in her facial features. Tom looked as if neither his clothes nor his skin fit properly. Perhaps he'd recently put on weight, but he didn't look as though he'd give a damn.

Lucy held up her platter. "Care for something?"

Ethan smiled at her, selecting a couple of delicious morsels and the napkins she offered.

"It's been too long," Magnus rumbled, taking another savory. He rolled his eyes at Lucy. "Like a son to me, yet too busy to make it home for my wedding. And now he invites himself on my honeymoon."

Juliette took her husband's arm. "The wedding was two months ago. And if this *was* our honeymoon, do you think I would agree to you going hunting for a week and leaving me all alone?"

"It's four days, my sweet. Three nights and four days. And you will have Lucy to keep you company."

Lucky Juliette, Ethan wanted to say. Instead he followed Magnus and Juliette over to a large sofa by the window, and answered his boss's questions about his flight and accommodations. That did not stop his eyes tracking Lucy as she served the other couples in the room. Her easy charm and bright smile drew a favorable response from men and women alike. Her pretty outfit floated around her body in a swirl of sea-greens and blues. She was light and grace, and impossible not to watch.

Juliette excused herself to freshen up before dinner. There was a moment's silence, then Magnus leaned forward. "She's something, isn't she?"

"Stunning," Ethan replied woodenly.

"I'm talking about our hostess," Magnus chuckled. "You haven't taken your eyes off her since you came in."

A jet of guilty pleasure whooshed up Ethan's breastbone, but he kept his voice casual. "A little young for me."

Magnus cleared his throat.

"Oh, Christ, Magnus. Sorry. I didn't mean…"

Magnus didn't appear to take offense. "That's all right, boy. I know I'm being tarred with your father's brush, and I can't blame you for it."

Ethan's hand curled into a fist in his lap. The way his mother had been discarded like yesterday's news after the old man had struck it lucky still burned. After ten years—more—of slave labor and biting poverty. Just tossed aside for a younger model. He could forgive his father some things. Not that.

He took a deep breath and rested his hands on his thighs. "What do you really know about her, Magnus?"

"All I need to know. She makes me happy. I know some folk think I'm a silly old fool. I didn't expect to find this sort of thing again. I've been on my own more than a dozen years, Ethan."

"I know," Ethan murmured, remembering the day of Theresa Anderson's funeral. "I wish you all the best, you know that."

"Thank you, Ethan."

He wouldn't push it tonight. He had little to go on anyway. Now wasn't the time.

"Actually I'm here on business, Magnus. I have a proposal and I didn't want to wait."

Magnus watched his wife re-enter the room. "Tomorrow, I think. No business tonight."

Juliette sat and began whispering into her husband's ear. "Are you coming in to dinner?" Magnus asked.

Ethan stretched. "Do you mind if I don't? I'm beat."

Tom seemed to have disappeared, along with all but one of the other couples. Lucy wiped glasses behind the bar. He excused himself and approached.

"You've lasted well for someone with jet lag. More wine?"

He nodded when she held up a bottle of chardonnay. "Half a glass. Think I'll call it a night."

She looked surprised. "Aren't you going in to dinner with the others?"

"No. These were delicious." He indicated the depleted platter of food. "Are you the chef?"

She shook her head. "If you get hungry in the night, just call room service."

He raised an eyebrow. "If I get hungry at three in the morning, you'll bring me a sandwich?"

A slight flush tinged her cheeks, telling him she wasn't slow on the uptake.

"Chef leaves around midnight, I'm afraid. Anyway, it's bad for the digestion to eat at that time of the day."

There was no mistaking the voluptuous lilt of her voice or the sparkle in her eyes. Ethan was enjoying himself. He must have tipped over into holiday mode earlier than the usual couple of days it took for him to unwind.

"I'll remember that," he said somberly, "and confine my appetite to chef's hours." He leaned back a little, and saw Tom re-enter the room. "Come show me the hunting gallery."

She put her tea towel down and accompanied him to the alcove. Hunting did not interest him in the slightest, but it was no hardship to be in close proximity to Lucy as she explained that wapiti were what North Americans call elk, and that thar and sika were different varieties of deer found here. He learned they were in the roar, or mating season. This was the preferable time to hunt because the animals were endowed with impressive antlers which dropped off after the season. Why else would Magnus, a keen trophy hunter, be here now?

There were ample photos in the alcove of successful hunters astride their kills, which included mountain goats and wild pigs. But what he enjoyed most was Lucy's evident pride in the magnificent landscape as she pointed to locations she had ridden to or picnicked at.

They were alone in the bar now, except for Tom.

Everyone else had retired to bed or gone through to the restaurant.

"You didn't say you knew the Andersons," she commented.

"You didn't ask." He shrugged. "First time I've met his wife. His wedding was—unexpected."

Tom approached, having cleared the tables. "I must apologize for the welcome you received today."

Ethan cocked a brow at him, noting that Lucy took a step back.

"It was not up to our usual high standard, I assure you."

Lucy half turned away, pursing her lips. Darn Tom. Why did he have to make a song and dance about everything? No doubt Ethan would have forgotten the whole thing if Tom hadn't brought it up.

She felt herself flush deeply at Tom's next missive. "A series of unfortunate incidents regarding vehicles— and my sister's poor timekeeping, I'm afraid."

Her heart sank.

"Was she late?" Ethan's quick response jolted her in mid cringe. "I'm afraid I was so charmed by your sister, I barely noticed the time or the transportation."

"Oh. Well, that's very generous of you." Tom sounded a little strained.

Lucy glowed with delight from the top of her head to her toes. What a nice thing to say—and how smooth. Tom was not going to like being put in his place like that one little bit, and she would no doubt have to pay for it. But for now, she reveled in the pleasure of approbation. She charmed him. Of course she did.

She could barely contain herself from skipping as all three walked to the bar, but she did manage a grateful grin at her champion.

"If there is anything we can do," Tom continued, "to make your stay with us more comfortable…"

Ethan glanced at Tom briefly, then returned his gaze to her. "Any chance of organizing a fax in my room?"

Lucy nodded. "I'll get on it first thing in the morning." She gave him a warm smile that she hoped conveyed the gratitude she felt. It was not often someone stuck up for her. She wanted him to know she was aware of it, and thankful.

Not just thankful. Absurdly pleased.

He smiled back. After a minute, Tom took a step back, huffing about clearing up.

"Goodnight, Lucy." Ethan threw a nod at Tom. "Tom."

"Sleep well."

She reluctantly turned back to Tom as he wiped the top of the stone bar. It had been a shock to discover earlier that Ethan was the vice-president of Magnus Anderson's company. Tom was fit to be tied, frantic in case she'd said anything inappropriate. The slight undertone of flirting on the way here did not worry her—to her mind it was mutual and harmless. But she could possibly have been more—deferential or something. Tom had a real bee in his bonnet about Magnus and his precious club.

"I told you he was cool about it."

"It's not the point. I need you to pick your socks up. No more fiascos like today. This is a five-star operation, and our guests don't want excuses. They want professional courtesy. Excellent facilities. Punctual service."

Exasperation, something she rarely gave in to, bubbled to the surface. "You should have confirmed the time. That's our deal. And do you think I can just conjure up vehicles out of nowhere?"

He scowled. He was a big man, like their father, but lately he had appeared more beefy than powerful.

"We need the club, Lucy. We cannot afford *not* to be on the Global List."

She rolled her eyes. "Seems to me we'd be a lot busier if we were allowed to advertise in the normal places, instead of just the stupid list."

"The Global List is regarded as one of the top three accommodation publications in the world. I don't think you appreciate the honor it is to be included."

Lucy privately thought it was a bit high-handed of the club to demand exclusive advertising rights. "Honor is all very nice, Tom, but it won't pay the bills, and you do seem worried about money all of a sudden."

"Which is something you have never given the slightest thought to," Tom retorted. "Swanning off all over the world for years with your hand out."

That stung, even as she recognized the truth in it. She loved traveling, and goodness knows she hadn't been wanted around here since her mother had left. But the moment she'd heard of her father's stroke, she had come home.

Never mind that it served as a timely escape from a tricky entanglement.

And when Tom had asked, she was only too pleased to help him with the business. But the truth was, she didn't really care about the lodge. Of course she would hate to see it fail, but her love was the forty thousand acres of countryside. Her birthright—and Tom's.

"I'm sorry for that, and I'll do anything I can to help."

Trouble was, with the life she had led so far, she didn't know how much help she would be.

"Anything?"

She touched his hand, feeling sorry he'd had to carry this burden alone. "Anything. You're really worried, aren't you?"

"I am. If you want to help, I'd like you to think about selling the land. Part of it, anyway."

Lucy jerked her hand back. "The land? Our land?"

"Lucy, since the farm manager quit a year ago, I've let the farm run right down. Half the stock that's left is wild. And the rest I pay next door to drench and move. We either need the farm to pay its own way or get the money for it. Otherwise how will we keep this place up to scratch?"

She could hardly believe her ears. Foreboding, deep and menacing, hollowed out her stomach. "What's going on, Tom? Why are things so bad?"

He turned away from her, his shoulders slumped. "It's a downturn in the market, that's all. We have to be prepared to explore other options."

"I'd sell the lodge before the land any day," she declared. "This is farming country. It's McKinlay farming country."

"It's a last resort, Lucy. Let's hope it doesn't come to that. We have to make sure Magnus has a great hunt and his wife has an equally good time." He turned off the lights to the bar and stood at the door, impatiently waving her through.

"You wouldn't… You can't be serious." How could he drop a bombshell like that and then just expect her to go to bed? She stalked past him, fingers of agitation squeezing her throat.

"And try to organize a tour or something for Rae," Tom ordered, his imperious voice riling her further. "I don't like the idea of him sniffing around while I'm on the hunt."

"Perhaps I should give him a tour of me," she told him snippily. "I could seduce him. Get him on our side that way."

She almost laughed at her half brother's shock.

"You will not! You'll keep your distance and be totally professional with that guy. I know his type—all business. He'd eat you for breakfast."

Lucy turned her back on him. "Man, I wish I knew what was bugging you lately." She shot him a scowl as she stomped off down the hall. "I was joking."

"I mean it, Lucy," Tom called after her. "Keep away from Rae. He's dangerous."

Three

Lucy rose in the half light, too restless to sleep. As was her custom when she stayed at Summerhill, she put her swimsuit on under a warm track suit, tossed a towel around her shoulders and skipped downstairs and out to the pool. It was just past six-thirty and she expected to have the pool to herself, but, to her dismay, she had been superseded.

A dark-haired figure made short work of the thirty-three-meter pool, long powerful arms scything effortlessly through the water.

Yes. She had wondered if he might be a swimmer or long-distance runner. Ethan would not lift weights or play a stop-start team sport. His body had the long clean lines that epitomised endurance, power with leashed—as opposed to explosive—energy.

She watched from the door as he executed a perfect turn: sleek, smooth, long-reaching. Lucy could not tear her eyes away and just as she was about to step fully into the room, Tom's comment of the night before came back to her. *Keep away…. He's dangerous.*

The whole upsetting conversation returned and she backed away.

It was necessary to release some tension, get moving. If swimming was out, an early-morning ride was the next best thing. Ten minutes later she exited the house and walked quickly to the stables. Monty, her horse, nickered in greeting. She lifted the pail of water to his gray nose and dug a couple of sugar cubes, filched from the breakfast tables, from her pocket.

"Monty the Monster," she chanted as she saddled him. He tossed his head and nudged her, looking for more sugar. "Frisky today." Lucy raised the pail again. He'd need a drink. She intended to use him hard.

They set off into the cool, dim morning, the struggling sun unable to pierce the clouds. The first part of the trail was tricky, especially in the dawn light. But about half an hour up, the trail planed out into a fast ride along the top of the huge gorge that ringed the valley. And when Monty took that final step up out of the scree and thistle and onto the plateau she pulled him up, patting and talking for a minute, and then gave him his head.

"Go boy, go!"

Lucy hunched forward, every muscle in her body screaming. Cold tears stung her cheeks. Her mouth twisted in concentration and velocity and her eyes squeezed into thin slits. Her Polar Fleece cap protected her ears, and sheepskin-lined gloves ensured her fingers were not stiffened with the cold.

"Ha! Good fella!" she yelled, her legs jammed hard into the horse's flanks.

They raced just a few feet from the lip of the gorge

that sliced the land down sixty or seventy meters to the river below. This gorge ringed Thunderstrike Valley for as far as the eye could see, across to the great Southern Alps.

When it was over, they slumped, heads hanging, breathing in great gulps of freezing air. Her cheek rested on the steaming neck of the animal for a minute or more until the horse moved restlessly. Then she roused herself and slid shakily down.

She loosened Monty's saddle and drew a grubby scrap of towelling from the saddlebag, rubbing the horse's chest and sides briskly. He seemed intent on backing away from her toward a patch of greenery. She tugged him over to a big overhang of rock. It crouched like a frog, ten meters from the edge of the gorge. Boulders and shrubs of prickly, yellow-flowered gorse clustered at its base. There was an opening that you could not see unless you stood directly in front of it.

Her special place.

She pulled off her hat and looped the reins over Monty's neck, leaving him to fossick through the tussock for food.

Stiff-arming a clump of gorse, she bent slightly and moved fully into the aperture. There was a large flat rock, fully three square meters and slightly elevated, so the view was unhindered above the foliage at the entrance. And the view was spectacular.

Her mother had sometimes brought her here as a child, placing her in front of her on the saddle. Lucy remembered the smell of her, her mother's long hair tickling Lucy's face, the thrill of clinging to the horse, as it climbed almost vertically up the steep cliff.

"I spy, with my little eye—" her childish voice would ring out in the semicave "—something beginning with…"

She'd help unwrap the sandwiches they had brought. They would play for hours. Once they'd been caught in a storm. Her mother pulled her well back into the cave and held her close, pressing her head into her bosom. But Lucy wasn't having it. "I want to see!" She squirmed and managed to ease her head around to watch the tongues of electricity lashing the valley. She exulted at the show, but her mother had trembled.

Now, a watery sun eased out of the dawn, and the early winter snowcaps of the mountains were hidden in thick pearl clouds. It was so quiet, the silence surged at her. She strained to see the snaking river below. Her eyes prickled and blurred, like the mist that snagged on the tops of the trees on the foothills.

She could not lose this. Her whole aimless existence came down to this, the panorama laid out in front of her. She had carried it all over the world inside her, and it far surpassed any landscape she had seen. Somehow, this view intermingled with her need to belong. Her last resort.

In truth, she knew that the times up here with her mother were the last times she had felt truly cherished. Had felt lovable.

Monty nickered and blew and was answered in kind. Alarmed, Lucy craned her neck around the gorse in time to see Ethan Rae dismount from Tilly, one of Summerhill's mares. A jolt of pleased agitation surged through her. Would this man not leave her in peace?

Ethan walked straight up to Monty and placed a confident hand on the gelding's neck.

Fighting a wild urge to stay hidden, Lucy slid along on her bottom to the entrance, then stood, using her arm to brush back the gorse. She didn't want him to worry. "How did you find your way up here?" she called.

His dark head snapped up and swiveled to find her. Was it pleasure causing her blood to race in her veins, or irritation at being disturbed while in an emotional mood?

"Followed you when you left the pool." He turned his back momentarily to loop his mare's reins around her neck and give Monty another pat.

As he approached, he made a thorough perusal of her warm sheepskin jacket and riding boots over black denims. "Beautiful place."

Lucy nodded. "My special place."

"Can see why."

She noticed he was still looking at her rather than the view. "I used to come up here with my mother."

Lucy tugged off her gloves, tossed them down and dug her bare hands deep into her pockets. Without invitation, he sat himself down on her rock. It was a big rock with more than enough room for two, but she remained on her feet. Somehow sharing her rock in this place, her special place, seemed too…intimate. Especially with someone who tickled her hormones the way he did.

If he had even an inkling of the thoughts racing through her mind, he seemed at ease with it. He made himself comfortable and peered up at her. "Are you like your mother?"

She kicked her toe into a tussock. "Physically." Too much, she thought. She nearly smiled, remembering Ellie's screams, as if there'd been a murder, when she'd found Lucy in the kitchen, scissors in hand and a pile of silvery locks slithering around her feet.

"Are you close?"

Lucy felt her mother's hands in her hair, braiding it. Remembered the smell of the rose-scented lotion she liked to wear. "I thought so."

There were many happy memories. All the neighboring farms got together and helped each other at busy times. The big old table in the dining room was often crammed to over-capacity, and elbows cracked and nudged. Loud and raucous laughter rang out, exciting the array of dogs banished to the step. And Thomas would be at the head of the table, louder and happier than everyone.

"I haven't seen her since she left."

He raised his dark brows.

"I was eight," she told him. "She ran off with one of the cowhands." She folded her arms around herself. "She was twenty years younger than Dad," she told him, as if to qualify it.

In the pause that followed, Lucy felt a confusing disquiet that she had just divulged her mother's true behavior to a virtual stranger. It had long been her way to make up the most extravagant fairy tales to her foreign friends. Her loving indulgent parents. Wonderful home-life. Mother-daughter shopping excursions to London and Paris.

Somehow it seemed wrong to lie here, in this place. Maybe it was because it was not only the last place she had felt lovable, but also honest.

Ethan nodded. "He never remarried?"

"No. It knocked the stuffing out of him."

Belle's defection had stunned the small community where the McKinlays were practically royalty. Thomas McKinlay was a big man in the district. Many had warned him about taking such a young bride.

"You were close to your father?" he asked.

Lucy considered. Close? After his stroke, he could hardly tell her he didn't want her around. When her mother had left, so had he in a sense. His withdrawal from her was nearly complete, as if she wasn't worthy of his regard. "Not really. Not since I was little." She shrugged and turned away. "I looked too much like Mum."

Cutting her hair short hadn't changed anything. Not in her father's embittered eyes. "It wasn't his fault. He was heartbroken. Humiliated. Before he had the stroke six months ago, I hadn't really been home, except for the odd weekend, since I was sent away to boarding school."

She liked it that he didn't mutter trite platitudes. Why should he care that her parents hadn't loved her?

"Were you good at school?"

Distracted by his interest, she eased down onto the rock, careful to keep plenty of distance between them. "Terrible." She grinned. "I mean, really."

"Academically or behaviorally?"

"Both. I'm dyslexic."

Ethan blew out a long breath. "Not a hanging offence."

She pointed her pert nose in the air and put on an aristocratic tone. "Not allowed at *my* school. It didn't happen to high-class, privately educated 'gels' like me. And we dyslexics became expert at covering it up."

"How?"

"By being naughty, of course," Lucy replied promptly.

Like most dyslexics, she had mastered any number of ways to cover up her disability so as not to be singled out as different. Usually, this involved getting into trouble or charming people. She laughed a lot, chattered a lot and found that teachers and schoolmates overlooked homework not done, exams failed or not attended.

"Not one teacher tried…?"

"Listen, I was rich. I suppose they thought I'd be all right. We high-class 'gels' are only biding our time till our posh wedding to some rich guy anyway, right?" She laughed. "Who needs education?"

Ethan drew his knees up and wrapped his arms around them. "Yesterday—you said you'd mixed up the times."

Lucy rolled her eyes. Because of his reaction last night, she didn't feel embarrassed. "See, it seems perfectly logical to someone like me to take the seven out of seventeen hundred hours and translate that to 7:00 p.m."

He nodded, a smile tugging the corner of his mouth. "Of course. My fault."

She liked him for saying that, even though it wasn't true. Then she remembered who he worked for. "You don't have to worry, Ethan. Tom takes care of all the office stuff, the bookings and so on. Yesterday was just a misunderstanding. It was me that goofed."

He held up his hands. "Not worried."

A faint pole of yellow light slanted between them from the entrance, distracting her. She pushed herself to her feet. "The sun's arrived."

Ethan watched her walk away to stand at the edge of the gorge. "Poor little rich girl" went through his mind. Beauty, money, prestige. But it wasn't all roses in this garden of Eden. Dyslexic. Cut off from the love she craved, the love of her parents. Maybe, he thought, the two of them were not so different after all.

Except that she still found it within herself to be loyal toward her jerk of a brother and compassionate in the face of her parents' indifference. Could he?

His own proud and aloof attitude toward his father

had never softened over the years. He had long ignored the resignation in his father's voice when Ethan once again cancelled a family dinner or rushed off ten minutes after arriving.

He knew he didn't have it in him, like Lucy, to be compassionate toward a man he had no respect for, purely because that man was his father.

"Look!" Her voice, girlishly excited, roused him. He rose from the rock and walked to her.

"A rainbow." She pointed out over the valley, squinting a little in the silvery haze.

Ethan exhaled, coming level with her. "You can see forever."

Lucy nodded and let her head loll back a little.

"Where does your place end?"

Her arm, still outstretched, made a long sweep. They stood at the head of the valley with the Alps at the far end. It was not a picture-perfect postcard; it was too rugged. The mountains jutted from the milky water of the winding river. Gouges, crude and immense, were hewn into closer, dun-coloured foothills that had their own kind of magnificence. Great swatches of dark, dull green denoted forest that halted and then started up again without any sort of order.

He could barely take it all in. The vision seemed magnified, too big for a country the size of New Zealand. A long-buried scrap of wonder rose up from his jaded mind and soared from the bottom of the far-off rainbow, which curved down to kiss the silvery rock, to the hazy tips of the mountains.

It was another world from the one he knew. He was used to taming land. It was his profession. But the lands that attracted tourists were calm and tranquil places. There was no calmness here, it was savage in parts.

He was reminded of his childish pledge, at the age of twelve, that one day he would farm. The land he had grown up on was cruel, endless and dry, spirit-sapping. He and his father had not been good enough to save it. Somehow he had always wanted to put that right.

And his time was coming, he knew. Once Turtle Island was done and dusted, he would have the rest of his life to search for the perfect piece of land, the perfect wife and set about proving he could be a better farmer, husband and father than his own father had been.

The vista soared and roared. He turned to look at Lucy. The wind, stronger here at the edge, lifted her pale hair toward the weak sun. It sparkled and he could not help himself—he who maintained control in every situation, who never lost sight of his goals. He reached out and touched her hair and she turned to face him with a soft cry of surprise that was stolen by the fitful breeze.

It almost burned him, the look on her face of pride and ownership and fierce love for this land of hers. She was part of it. She was nature, but not in a robust way— more childlike. The blue haze of the mountains shone in her eyes. The silver of scree and rock were mirrored in her hair. She moved with the graceful sway of the trees. She would change with the seasons and the ebb of the atmosphere, and he admired that—wanted that— because he and his father had failed so abysmally.

Entranced, he moved toward her, wondering if she realized that he was going to kiss her. His fingers laced through her hair. His other hand pulled on the side of her open jacket, his eyes on hers, clearly signaling his intention.

She did not step back, although her arms seemed to clamp to her sides.

Oh yes, I am going to kiss you, Lucy McKinlay,

right or wrong. It was a rare moment in Ethan's life. He knew he'd spend a lifetime wondering if he did not go with the instinct driving him right now.

His mouth descended onto hers and the first touch of her slowed him down. There was no hurry. If he had to do this, he would do it properly.

With his tongue he traced the shape of her small mouth, lingering in the bow in the center of her top lip. Cool in the morning chill, and incredibly soft. He coaxed her lips apart and thought of nature—cold morning air, snow on your tongue, fresh-cut grass. The swirling sea-colors of her outfit last night as she moved around the bar, bending and straightening, smiling and chatting. That vision had kept him awake for most of the night, so restless that he was compelled to take an early-morning swim. And to knock himself out trying to impress her when he saw her at the door to the pool.

Lucy's mouth kissed back, warming and accepting. Her tongue did not shy from his, her breath shuddered into his mouth. Her hair was as soft and fine as he had ever felt. His fingers threaded through it, discovering the shape of her skull, making her gasp when he massaged the base of it. He wanted more, but it wasn't so much carnal or wanting to go farther, as it was just to continue. The taste of her, the feel of her skin, it all combined into a whole delicious addictive feast.

But her arms were rigid at her sides. It was that fact that pricked his comprehension, brought him back through the clouds. His hands moved to her shoulders and ran lightly down her arms, as if to thaw their stiffness. He leaned back slightly, a little breathless but wanting to see her response.

Her eyes remained closed. She captured her bottom lip with small white teeth and drew it into her mouth, inhaling. Then her eyes opened and slowly focused on him.

Heavy-lidded and fringed by light-brown lashes that seemed longer at the outer corners, there was real depth in those lovely blue eyes. Surprise. Embers of heat going up in a little shower of sparks. He'd thought her unresponsive. Afraid, even, when he'd felt the tension in her arms. She wasn't. A strong tremor rolled through her slender body, still pressed up against his. She was holding back, but she was as affected as he was. Her hands fisted and she pulled them back behind her, as if that might stop the trembling.

Lucy McKinlay might be innocent. She might even be a common gold digger. But he had never wanted to claim and tame someone so much.

"I—we—we'll be late for breakfast," she whispered and pulled dazedly from his embrace, took a couple of unfirm steps back.

As if waking from a dream, he squinted at her, wondering what on earth had just possessed him.

"I must get back." Distance had made her stronger, firmer.

She turned her back on him. He watched her walk to her horse, take some time inspecting the saddle, crooning to the animal. Her hat and gloves were next for a fastidious inspection before being tugged on—and all without looking at him once. Finally she mounted and nudged her horse with the slightest pressure of her legs and moved to Ethan's mare, leaning down to collect the reins. "Are you coming down now?"

He took the reins she held out and nodded curtly, telling himself he was relieved she did not want to talk about what had just occurred. He needed time to sort it out in his head. Not given to uncontrollable urges, he had to wonder if the magic of the landscape had somehow drugged him.

Four

Ethan had scheduled a meeting with Magnus after lunch. On the way to the conference facility, he paused by the front door to look out onto the veranda. Juliette lounged on a hammock-chair that rocked gently as she moved her crossed ankles in a lazy circular motion. She read aloud from a glossy brochure or magazine. Lucy listened from the bench seat, her bare feet tucked up under her.

From twenty feet away, she looked like anyone else. You had to get close to appreciate the silky radiance of her skin, the warmth and sparkle of her eyes.

Correction. You had to get close enough to touch her on a hilltop with a magical view to get really carried away. He was still shaking his head over his impetuous actions that morning. Perhaps it was the contrast between her and the type of women he usually came into contact with.

Women like Juliette.

His eyes narrowed as he studied the new Mrs. Magnus Anderson. Growing up in Australia, he was used to tanned and toned athletic girls. As he got older and traveled all corners of the world, he was confronted with more tanned and toned women, but with a subtle difference. They got their tan and their tone from the beauty parlor and the personal trainer.

Sleek and bronzed. Stylishly dressed. Immaculately made-up and coiffed. The perfect companion. He stared hard at her. What was she hiding? And what were her intentions toward Magnus?

With a start, he realised that Lucy was looking right at him. He met her eyes and all thoughts of Juliette were whisked away.

He did not smile in greeting. So they had a secret to share, a bit of a kiss when they'd only just met. Good sense told him to step back. It wasn't his style to deliberately hurt, confuse or treat women carelessly. With little time to socialize, he made sure his partners knew the score. No romance. No promise of anything more. The few women he dated were of similar disposition to him: ambitious, busy, on the way up with no time to spare.

There was something vulnerable about that doll-like mouth, something that both drew him to her and warned him off. She had not smiled and from where he stood, he could not read her expression. Then she nodded and turned back to Juliette.

Magnus was in an exuberant mood. Ethan tossed his briefcase on the table and poured himself a coffee, and for the next hour or so, they went through every detail of the successful completion of the Middle Eastern resort.

At the conclusion, Ethan stretched and stood to re-fill his cup. Magnus sorted the sheaf of papers in front of him and fussed in his top pocket for a cigar, which he clamped down on enthusiastically. It was in defer-ence to his doctor, Ethan knew, that he only actually smoked one cigar a day, but he chomped through four or five others.

"Looking pleased with yourself," Ethan commented, resuming his seat.

Magnus removed the cigar and pointed it at him, his eyes twinkling. "It's marriage, my boy. You should try it."

Ethan considered again raising the subject of the newspaper clippings, but he hated to blight his boss's relaxed good humor. It could wait till they were back in Sydney. Or until he had something concrete from the P.I. "Just like a newlywed," he sighed. "You must try and fix up all your poor, miserable, single friends."

"Uh-huh." Magnus leaned back in his chair and squinted at him. "Got a bit of a light in your own eye today."

Ethan pushed the unbidden thought of Lucy firmly away. "There is something else." He pulled his open briefcase toward him, his mouth tightening into a cau-tious grin. The Turtle Island file was on top and he lifted it and placed it on the table. Magnus's big hand landed on the plain manila folder and he slid it closer, flipping back the cover.

While he studied the file, Ethan paced, savoring the anticipation of his boss's reaction. Turtle Island had historical significance to MagnaCorp. He counted on Magnus jumping at the chance to recoup a substantial loss suffered.

He sat down again, his hand threatening to drum up a tattoo of impatience on the table.

Finally Magnus cleared his throat, his head still bent but the last page of the slim file inching closed. He picked up his cigar, tapped the end of it on the table and brought it slowly to his mouth. The chair creaked as he shifted to face Ethan.

The older man's eyes were lit up with guarded pleasure. "When did you start on this?"

"Got the tip-off a month ago."

"You've been busy."

Ethan nodded. "I'm the only player. Clark knows."

Magnus eyed him, nodding slowly. "Clark's a good man."

Ethan leaned back in his own seat, folding his arms. "Is it a go?"

Magnus roused himself. "Your father—" He tapped the file. "He did all the work on this, twenty years ago. Would have clinched it, too, but for the coup."

Ethan sighed. The old man read him like a book. "Before my time."

He was well aware of the history. Nearly twenty years ago, before this priceless piece of land had been nationalized, there were only two companies in the Pacific large enough to buy the rights to develop the bay into the world's most exclusive resort. "You also spent millions," he reminded him. "Lawyers, surveyors, architects…"

"And we both lost."

"Here it is. You don't want it?"

"Hell, yes. It would be the jewel in my crown. I'd be thrilled for you if it wasn't *your* father and *this* island."

"It's business," Ethan told him stubbornly.

"You know, Ethan, you only took the job I offered you to rub his nose in it. Else you'd be running his corporation now, instead of mine. He'd welcome you, and it wouldn't be like working for someone else. You're his only son. His rightful heir."

"I've earned my money—sufficient, I think—my way."

"You've done well." Magnus pursed his mouth thoughtfully. "If you ever decide to call in ownership of all your units at the same time, you'd damn near break me."

They smiled at the joke. Magnus had been among the top five Australasians on the rich list for the last decade.

From the time Ethan had completed his first project for MagnaCorp, he'd deferred the generous bonuses his boss offered in lieu of a down payment on a small portion of land on every project since. Sometimes this took the shape of a unit to be let out, a small piece of beachfront. In one case, he'd purchased the resort golf course.

"I want you to think about this, long and hard. Jackson's done well these last few years, even if he didn't do right by you and your mother."

"My father doesn't even feature in my thoughts most of the time. Some families just aren't that close."

"Yes but his failures made you what you are today," Magnus insisted. "Forgive him, Ethan. Don't allow him to leave this world with regrets. You do, and you'll do the same."

Ethan blew out a long breath and leaned toward the table. He picked up the Turtle Island file and saluted his boss with it. "Duly noted. And appreciated. Now, can we get down to business?"

Magnus grinned. "I swear, I've never met anyone as single-minded as you. Loosen up, son. Quit ticking things off that interminable list in your head. Come hunting with us."

Ethan shook his head. "Not my idea of fun, old man. I'll stick around here, enjoy the scenery."

A smile nagged the corners of Magnus's mouth. "Little Miss Lucy does kind of light up a room, even in the middle of nowhere, doesn't she?" The smile broadened when he saw Ethan's guarded expression.

"Let me have a go at Turtle Island, Magnus," he hedged.

Magnus shook his head ruefully. "All right, son. If you think you can swing Turtle Island without causing an irretrievable break between you and your father, then go for it. I have every faith in you."

Ethan slapped the file on the table in elation. "I'll call Clark now, get the ball rolling."

Magnus waved his hand. "Since you'll be hanging around here, how about doing something for me? I've been hearing some disturbing things about Summerhill. It's why I chose this as a belated honeymoon."

"What sort of things?" Ethan's interest piqued.

"Cutbacks. Maintenance issues. The word is, they're close to the wall. The integrity of the club is paramount. There can be no hint of impropriety."

The reference to the club made Ethan smile. Now that Ethan managed most of the affairs of MagnaCorp, Magnus had slowed down some, but the club was his pet. "Sure. I'll ask a few questions. Looks okay, so far." Better than okay, he thought, almost giving a wolfish grin. Lucy's tantalizing presence could help him overlook just about anything. "The accommodation is spot-on, if a bit faded. Incredible location."

"Mmm. Keep your ear to the ground. And have a bit of a rest. I'll be back Wednesday, and we fly out on Friday." He stood slowly. "Keep tomorrow night free. Tom has offered us some tickets for New Zealand versus Argentina. One of his friends has a corporate box. Whad-dya say? It's compulsory to see a rugby game when in New Zealand."

Ethan closed his briefcase and picked up his jacket. "Who's coming?" he asked casually.

Magnus turned to the door, but not before Ethan caught a definite gleam in his eye. "My wife and I. You and Lucy. Sadly, Tom will be busy with arrangements for our safari. We'll have dinner afterwards and Lucy was going to see about booking a hotel in town for the night, save driving back."

Lucy allowed herself a small smile of satisfaction. Nothing had gone wrong for once. She had checked the Andersons and Ethan into their hotel and had had time to call in to the apartment and pick up her beloved New Zealand jersey. The real stroke of luck was finding a rare parking spot on the street not three blocks from the stadium. They would be seated in good time.

The atmosphere was festive as thirty-seven thousand people poured in through the gates. A fireworks display sent big puffs of smoke rolling across the field and into the stands. Lucy paused a minute—she loved fireworks—then noticed Ethan had stopped to turn and look at her.

She had planned to avoid him as much as politely possible for the duration of his stay and had managed that nicely since yesterday's incident on the gorge. But today they had all ganged up on her, even Tom. "Take my SUV," he'd insisted, when she'd protested that four would be a bit of a squeeze in the Alfa.

Ethan had turned back to say something to Magnus. A body bumped into her and she stepped aside, her eyes intermittently on the fireworks and Ethan's tall figure a few feet ahead. "Sorry," she murmured automatically, then felt someone grip her arm.

A face, clean-shaven and loose-looking, peered at her closely. Because of the crush behind, she strove to keep walking but his grip tightened.

"Ms. McKinlay."

A waft of strong alcohol preceded his words and she stiffened. The face looked vaguely familiar, but distaste muddled her memory. "I'm sorry, I…"

"Joseph Dunn. Friend of your brother's."

A small spurt of relief was wiped out by the realization that he still hung on to her arm. "Oh. Okay."

While she stammered, her eyes lifted over the man's shoulder and she saw Ethan frowning back at her.

"We met at the casino one night, not long after you came home."

Lucy did not remember but she did know his face. She tried to think of something to say to politely extricate herself from his grasp. "Nice to see you," she murmured, lifting her arm pointedly. To her confusion, he seemed to grip her harder. Giving up the pretence of politeness, she pulled against him. "Excuse me," she began icily.

"Where's your brother?" The fleshy lips were no longer smiling. It was as if he too had given up on diplomacy.

"Tom?" A little scared now, she registered that Ethan was pushing toward her, only a few feet away.

"Yes, Tom." The tone was now openly belligerent. "I know he's here. I saw his car."

Perhaps emboldened by rescue at hand, she tugged sharply to free herself.

"Hey!" She heard Ethan's voice crack through the din of the crowd. The man checked.

"What do you want?" she hissed.

He glanced quickly over his shoulder then his fingers dug deep into her arm, so hard that tears of pain and outrage sprang into her eyes. He shoved his face very close. "Tell him I'm looking for him." With that, he gave her a small but quite rough push.

A little dazed and off balance, she heard a louder "Hey!" close now, right in front of her, and then the tang of Ethan's aftershave blitzed the smell of alcohol and malice away. Her head cleared. He came level with her, moving determinedly in the direction of the departing man. Without thinking, Lucy raised her hand quickly. "Leave it!" She slapped her hand quite forcefully on his chest.

His wide chest.

His hard chest.

His heart beat strongly under her flat palm. He looked down at it, possibly surprised at the force she'd used or perhaps it was the commanding tone of voice. Then he looked at her face.

She stared back, trying to think of something to say. Her train of thought was completely attuned to the rhythm of his heart under her hand. And the warmth of his skin under the shirt invited each of her fingers to flex and flatten out, pressing fractionally closer.

"You okay? What did he…?"

Lucy gingerly took control of herself, lifting her hand off his chest. "He was just being vulgar." She started to walk in the direction he'd come from. "Come on, they'll be wondering."

Ethan's hand landed on her arm, the same arm. His grip was gentle, but his voice was not. "Lucy."

She tensed, inhaling deeply. This had to be handled with a light touch. She had no idea what that man had wanted with Tom, but her gut feeling was it had something to do with money.

Turning slowly to face him, she looked pointedly at his hand on her arm. "Gosh, it's my week for being manhandled." With satisfaction, she saw his eyes narrow at the coolness she'd imparted.

There were people everywhere, pushing impatiently to get to their seats. Ethan guided her determinedly to the side of the thoroughfare. When her back was against the wall, he leaned in close. His hands were on the wall on either side of her, cutting off her escape, but he did not touch her.

"What was that about?" His voice was low and tense.

Lucy quailed when she saw how tightly reined he was; his jaw was clamped, his eyes flashing. Why he was angry with her? "It was nothing."

His breath puffed over her face. "Ex-boyfriend?"

She shuddered. "No."

"His hands were on you."

She saw then it was not her he was angry with. God help Joseph Dunn if Ethan stumbled across him tonight. "As were yours, yesterday morning," she said carefully.

As a distraction, it worked. He shifted slightly, leaning on his arms, and his eyes slid down to her lips. A breathless shiver of excitement fizzed through her. Her fingers curled in remembrance of his heartbeat.

He was thinking of their morning kiss, as she was.

"Did I bully you yesterday morning?" he asked softly, and brought his eyes back to hers.

Smouldering voice. Smouldering eyes. Desire, not just excitement or anticipation but hot, flowing, knee-trembling desire rolled through every cell of her. And he saw it, recognized it. She saw his pupils dilate, his lips part slightly, and Lucy had to fight not to sag against him, helpless with longing.

And then the stadium erupted. Loudspeakers, applause, music rushed into the vacuum between them and sanity returned. Lucy shook her head and ducked quickly under his arm. "Forget it. Let's go." She made a timely escape, breathing deeply.

Ethan straightened. Following, he glared at the sea of people, as if to pick out the obnoxious man. "What did he want with your brother?"

She could not escape him; his long legs ate up the ground. "My brother? I told you, he was just trying it on. We'll miss kick-off."

She flicked him a nervous look and knew he saw right through her lie. He must have heard the man.

He moved to her side and put his arm through hers decisively. "You'll tell me later."

It sounded like a threat but she was somehow soothed by the touch of his arm running the length of hers.

This was a revelation. He was being protective, even territorial, of her. A champion. That was a first, ever since she'd been a kid, anyway. It was hard to know how to feel about it. No doubt she'd be called to account at some stage. By then, she hoped she'd have thought up something to distract him.

Several distractions went through her mind over the course of the game. The corporate box catered for about twenty but seemed to be well over-subscribed tonight. Magnus and Juliette had managed to snare a leaner and some stools right in front of the big glass doors, but it was a crush. Stuck in between Magnus and Ethan, she wrapped her arms around her torso and tried to diminish her size.

It was no good. The whole of her right leg was pressed up against his left. She felt on fire all down that side. If she moved to sip her drink, her elbow touched him. If he half turned to exchange a word with Magnus, his breath lifted strands of her hair. If she leaned forward to talk to Juliette, he seemed to fill the space behind so she could not lean back without touching him.

This attraction was fast becoming overwhelming, especially since her skin—her very nerve endings—were already sensitized by their altercation earlier. She was totally aware of every breath he took. Of every muscle in his long, taut thigh pressed against hers. He had rolled his shirt sleeves up a little and her eyes strayed, time and again, to the coffee-colored skin of his forearm with its sprinkling of springy-looking dark hair, and to his hands—long-fingered and spread wide on his thighs.

Worst of all was his reaction to the accidental touches. A stillness which told her more than the many three-second meetings of their eyes. A stillness that seemed to pass from him into her. An awareness of each other breathing, moving, just being. They spoke hardly at all, and the silences were fraught with a constant hum of excitement and perplexity.

What a relief to finally leave the small area and lose herself in other people again, although Ethan stuck quite close to her this time.

The crowd was in high spirits as they swept onto the streets. The plan was that Lucy would drop the Australians at their central hotel, go back to the apartment and change and meet them at the new jazz restaurant she'd booked, by ten or ten-thirty.

But when they came to the spot where Tom's SUV should have been, it was nowhere to be seen. Lucy knew she'd left it right here; she recalled seeing the black balloons fastened to the lamppost right beside where she'd parked.

Where a green Toyota now sat. She shook her head. "Good grief, it must be the next street over."

"Look." Juliette was looking at the ground, moving the toe of her expensive boot over the road. "Glass."

Ethan crouched. "Broken car-window glass." He picked up a fragment. "Someone broke into it and drove it away."

"I don't believe it." Lucy squatted beside him, rummaging in her bag for her phone. She was hot with embarrassment. What a great impression of her city this would leave on the visitors. "I'll call a cab."

It was handy having a few connections in the tourist business and five minutes or so later, a corporate cab pulled up alongside.

When they reached the hotel, Ethan got out to let Magnus and Juliette out and then insisted, despite her objections, on accompanying her to the police station.

Half an hour later, they were still in the queue and she was still objecting. It was a busy Saturday night with an assortment of drunks, assaults and reports of thefts to entertain them. Finally they stood in front of a young policeman and Lucy outlined why they were there.

"Fill this in." A form was placed on the counter. Her heart sank. Filling in forms on the spot with people watching—him watching—was as much fun as being in the dentist's chair. Both men's eyes on her, she picked up the pen and frowned down at the paper. Her face felt hot. The text in front of her danced behind her eyes.

"Registration number?" the officer inquired, tapping his keyboard.

Lucy wished the ground would open up and swallow her. In times of stress, her dyslexia was exacerbated.

She knew there was nothing wrong with her intellect, just the way her brain processed words and figures.

Right. And it didn't matter how often she heard those words, or read the literature from well-meaning disability learning centers. She felt so dumb, having to punch her PIN number in three times at the front of a queue, putting numbers back to front. Names, too—if she was given a written message to call someone she didn't know called Joe Brown, Lucy was likely to say, "Is that Brown Joe?" when the called person answered.

Then she felt Ethan's fingers cover hers, easing the pen from her iron grip.

"Call Tom," he murmured, his lips brushing her ear and making her shiver.

Vastly relieved, she pressed the speed dial on her phone. Tom answered on the third ring. Quickly she explained the situation and requested the car registration number.

Tom didn't respond. Someone in the queue behind muttered loudly about the time they were taking.

"Tom?" The growing worry must not show in her voice. Not with *him* standing there.

"I forgot to register it."

"What? When?" Her voice was low, her face turned away to hide her confusion.

Tom sighed heavily. "Last year."

"Last year?" She swallowed a very unladylike oath, snapped the phone off and slowly turned back to the cop, unwilling to face Ethan. "It appears he forgot to register it."

The cop looked disgusted.

"But you can still look for it, can't you?"

From the corner of her eye she saw Ethan lay the pen carefully on the counter and lift the form. His hand landed lightly on her shoulder. "I'd say your credibility's shot," he told her quietly. Turning, he coaxed her toward the exit, crumpling the form into a ball. They moved outside, Lucy glad of the cool night air on her burning face. Sighing miserably, she sank down on the bottom step leading into the station. Ethan remained standing, leaning against the wall of the building.

Lucy stared at his feet. "I can read and write, you know. It's just when I'm not prepared or people are watching, I get flustered."

He did not answer and she shot a look at his face. His expression was serious and concerned.

Then he moved, startling her. "Shove up." He sat down. "What was the name of the guy at the stadium?"

"I—don't know," she lied and then put her head in her hands. What was going on with Tom? They'd never been close, but they were family. His recent moods and the problems he kept alluding to were beginning to really worry her.

"Why are you covering up for him?"

"Who?"

"Your brother."

"I'm not."

"Lucy, he sent clients out in an unregistered vehicle, which was subsequently stolen, probably by a disgruntled associate."

"We don't know that."

"I heard the guy. He'd seen the car and you're to tell Tom he's looking for him."

Could this night get any worse? Lucy searched the streets, trying desperately to think of a way to deflect him. "My, Grandma. What big ears you have."

They were interrupted by a couple trying to pass. Ethan rose and Lucy pressed close to the railing to let them through. He put his hands in his pockets and stared down at her. "What sort of trouble is Tom in?"

She pushed herself to her feet. "He's not. Let's get to the restaurant. You've wasted enough time on me tonight."

He just stood there, looking at her. "I have time to waste."

Silence, and that peculiar stillness, rolled between them. After the evening spent pressed up against him, being so aware of him, and being in no doubt that he felt the same, it was tempting, *so* tempting, to give in, twine her arms around his neck and forget her problems for the rest of this night.

She was experiencing this way too much today. It was hard to recall they had met only a couple of days earlier. There was a familiarity and intensity that was usually reserved for more…intimate acquaintances.

Breaking eye contact, she took the last step down. "Ethan, I'm sure that person had nothing to do with the car. But I'll tell Tom, and then it's his decision if he wants to involve the police. Satisfied?"

Her pulse leapt when he sought her eyes and swept her with a rare, reluctant smile, his dark brows arched.

Lucy shook her head and began to walk away from temptation.

His voice behind her made her check. "One condition."

She looked back over her shoulder at him.

"Magnus and Juliette are on their honeymoon." He drew level with her. "So let's you and I leave them to it and have a drink."

Five

"Unless," he continued, "you'd rather go home."

Lucy blinked at him, swallowing hard. Images of being alone together, enclosed within four walls, with a bed not too far away, leapt between them.

"Uh—I think there's a bar around here somewhere." Her eyes slid away and he smiled. A drink would do, for now.

They jostled their way to the bar at a noisy pub a couple of blocks away. The only perch was outside, leaning on a forty-four-gallon barrel with the smokers, nursing their beers. Ethan pulled his jacket closer around his neck.

"Shouldn't you call Magnus and tell them not to wait for us?"

Ethan shook his head. He'd already told Magnus that when they'd dropped them off. Reporting a crime on a Saturday night when there was a big game on in town would have been a long job.

Lucy was quiet, and, although he badly wanted to know what was going on with her brother, he thought he'd let her loosen up with some friendly chitchat first.

He sipped from his bottle and followed her gaze to a young couple leaning on their own drum a few feet away. There was some pretty heavy kissing going on there. It amused him when Lucy turned back and shifted so she was facing away from them.

"Why aren't you hunting with the others tomorrow?" She took the slice of lemon from the neck of the beer bottle and raised it to her nose, inhaling deeply.

He shook his head distastefully. "Not into blood sports."

"Why not?"

He sighed. "As a kid, my job was to shoot or cut the throats of the animals on our farm."

"Why?"

"They were starving."

"Why?" she repeated.

"Drought." Ethan bared his teeth mirthlessly. "My father and I were piss-poor farmers."

A movement caught his eye and they both glanced over at the couple again. The guy had put his fingers in the girl's waistband and pulled her lower body flush against his. Their kisses were deep. They kept breaking off to talk, but all the time he was tugging her gently into the front of him.

"Where was this?" Lucy asked, bringing him back.

"Western Australia."

"How old were you?"

"Moved to the farm when I was six. Walked off it at twelve."

"Are you an only child?"

He nodded.

"When did the drought end?"

Ethan shrugged. "We left when the bank foreclosed. Moved into a trailer park in Perth." He narrowed his eyes at her. "Nosy, aren't you?"

She nodded, not in the least self-conscious. "Are your parents still together?"

"He kicked my mother out when I was thirteen."

Lucy's eyes widened. He could almost hear her mind ticking over. Maybe they had something in common. Lonely children, dysfunctional families…

"Kicked her out for a girl five years older than me. She was only interested after he won the state lottery. Trailer trash no more." He raised his bottle and clinked hers in a salute.

She stared at him, fiddling with the stud in her ear. Women, he thought wryly. Nothing fascinated them more than someone's troubles.

"What happened to your mum?"

"Came back to New Zealand. She's from Kaikohe."

"Why?"

His brows rose.

"I mean, why did she leave *you?*" She had said exactly what was in her mind, judging by the hand she clamped to her mouth. Ethan nearly laughed out loud. A blush streaked her cheeks. She was embarrassed, but she wanted to know. That was the sort of thing women liked to know.

He looked at her seriously for a moment. "Farming the outback's tough for a woman. After the farm, he drank and she worked. Couldn't afford a school uniform, so she home-schooled me in between cleaning jobs. Then one day, my father spent his last dollar on the lottery and it came in. I was sent to a private school. They bought a big house. Mum stopped work, got her hair done." He took a long pull on his bottle, enjoying the total concentration on Lucy's face. It was no hardship being the object of her avid attention.

Where was he? "Might have been a lousy farmer, the old man, but turned out he was lucky as sin on the share market. Doubled his money in little more than a year." He set his bottle down very carefully. "And that's when the fortune hunters started sniffing around."

It was the longest speech he had made. Lucy looked riveted. He decided to give her a bit of a jolt, so he hit her with the full intensity of his eyes. "Young, beautiful women who'd do anything for money." His voice was low and loaded. "You know the type."

He watched her blink, as if surprised, then her head nodded once, slowly, as if something had suddenly clicked in her mind.

Was she a gold digger, he wondered? He swore he could see no guile in her eyes, though it was dark out here. But a couple of her lighthearted quips had stuck under his collar like grit.

And yet, there was a freshness about her that did not equate with any of the parade of girls his father traded in at the rate of one every couple of years. Or the women who schmoozed in the corporate world he moved in. He couldn't imagine anyone more different.

"I was settled in a good school. I guess she didn't want to disrupt my schooling any more than it had been. I spent every holiday with her."

"What happened to you after she left?" Lucy asked.

He considered. "Did well at school. Made the national swim team."

"I knew it," she smiled. "I thought you looked like a swimmer."

"Could have made the Olympics."

"But?"

Another long pause while he assessed how much more to divulge. He wasn't one for baring his soul but he felt easy, comfortable. Burning up for her, sure, but enjoying himself and quite prepared to continue. "Wasn't part of the plan."

"The plan?" Lucy shifted against the barrel.

"To—succeed. No luck involved."

"To succeed where your father failed," she told him triumphantly.

He grinned at the sparkle in her eyes. "Dammit, you're right, Freud!"

"You haven't forgiven him, have you?" Her head was cocked to one side, the grin fading.

"Have you forgiven your parents?"

Lucy's mouth twisted, just for a moment. Her thumb knuckle pressed on her chin. "I don't suppose it's easy being a parent." She smiled sadly. "If I ever get the chance, I'll know what *not* to do."

"I'll drink to that," Ethan said, raising his bottle and toasting her. "Here's to making a better job of it."

They clinked bottles.

"Would you like to see your mother again?"

Lucy picked at the label of her bottle. "No." She shook her head. "She made her choice and obviously I didn't figure."

"She was walking from your father, not you."

Her smile held a gentle rebuke. "Oh, Ethan. If that were the case she would have kept in touch, like your mother."

She inhaled deeply then looked up at him seriously. "But I do regret that I let Dad get away with ignoring me all those years. If I'd tried a bit harder…"

"Maybe if *he'd* tried a bit harder," he told her and

there was an edge to his voice. Why should she feel bad about it? It was she who had been treated shabbily.

Where was this coming from, this protective thing he had going on here? He'd always been a loner, proud of it. Had no problem with the strongest-of-the-pack-survive rule.

"You have to forgive them, don't you?" she was saying. "They're family, and you only get one."

He frowned. "I think that's—generous, considering what your parents did."

She lifted her shoulders in a shrug. "What's the point in being bitter?"

Ethan found that interesting. He would not have described himself as bitter. But it had never occurred to him that his father deserved forgiveness. Hell, if that were the case, what did his poor mother deserve?

And then the thought popped into his mind that his mother had been perfectly happy, these last ten years. His father had been generous with the settlement and she had a nice spread and seemed happy with Drako, her boy-toy up north.

"Actually—" she broke into his thoughts, and her tone was much lighter "—if you want to think about it, we've got quite a lot in common. My mum married a much older man, then took off with a younger one. Your dad likes younger women. Just think what our combined gene pool would produce."

Ethan had already started laughing at her words. But when Lucy realized what she'd said, the look of shock that crossed her face really did him in. That's when he threw back his head and let rip.

Her hand was clamped over her mouth again but as he laughed she relaxed. Her elbows rested on the barrel and she leaned on them, shading her eyes.

"Don't worry about me," Ethan chuckled. "Just say exactly what's on your mind."

She shook her head, still hiding her eyes, but she was smiling ruefully. "I can't believe I said that." She sighed. "Strike that from the record."

He cleared his throat, still grinning. It felt good— great. He couldn't remember the last time he'd shared a good laugh with a woman. Man, she was cute.

"I'm sorry. Tom's always saying I need to engage brain before mouth."

Their smiles faded. Tom seemed to have that effect. "You're very loyal," Ethan said quietly, and watched a mini slide-show of expression on her face. From humor to caution in one second. She would be hopeless at poker. "Your brother doesn't know how lucky he is."

Lucy pursed her lips. "And have you succeeded? With your success plan?"

He decided to let her get away with changing the subject. He was having a good time. Why waste it on Tom McKinlay? "Nearly," he answered. "A couple of things on the list still to be ticked off."

"Don't stop now," she encouraged him.

"Kissing you again is right at the top," he murmured, holding her gaze.

He heard the little catch in her throat. She glanced at him then away. And he was amused to see she focused on the couple swallowing tongues for quite awhile this time. Only that's not all they were doing. The boy's knee was right between the girl's legs now and there was some pretty suggestive rubbing going on. Lucy was blushing prettily when she eventually turned back to him.

"But I think you know that," he continued in the same teasing tone.

"Oh," was all she had to say, and she wouldn't meet his gaze.

The air seemed to crackle in his ears. He could not recall ever being so aware of a woman. This whole night had been one long exercise in self-restraint. Not just his sexual self-restraint, although that was compelling after being pressed up against her for the duration of a rugby game. But keeping it loose had not been easy when he knew she was lying about the slob who'd shoved her. And it would take some time to forget the shame burning in her eyes when faced with completing a simple form. Lucy McKinlay touched him in ways he had not expected.

She had stopped ravaging the bottle label. It blew in long strips around the rim of their barrel. Instead, the bottle's neck was being strangled in a white-knuckled fist. Finally she put it down between them with a sharp rap and frowned.

"Ethan, you're a client. I have to keep things on a professional level."

Ethan snorted. "Hardly a doctor-patient relationship."

She looked heavenward but did raise a smile. "I'm not saying I'm not tempted, but…I'm trying really hard…."

He waited.

She sighed heavily, obviously uncomfortable. "Just— nothing's going to happen between us. Not while you're a guest at Summerhill."

He squinted at her. "I move out of Summerhill and into a hotel, you'll go out with me?"

A resigned laugh bubbled up in her throat. "No! Not while Magnus and Juliette are here. Maybe not ever."

He shook his head. "Not ever's a long time, Lucy."

"I've known you two days," she pointed out reasonably.

"Yeah." Ethan nodded. "Surprised me, too." He stroked his chin and saw that her eyes followed the movement. "I don't take enough holidays."

"All business?" Her tone was gentle but it sounded like a taunt.

"You're the one trying to be professional."

She broke eye contact and rubbed her forehead. He swore any professional thoughts were blasted away when she copped an eyeful of the young lovers. The girl was practically riding the guy's leg—her feet were all but off the ground. They both watched shamelessly. When Lucy finally dragged her eyes back to his, he met and held her gaze for long seconds. Brazen images—bare skin, mouths seeking, frantic touching—danced behind his eyes and were mirrored in hers.

She swept up the fallen strips of label distractedly and stuffed them down the throat of her empty bottle. "Will you be here when Juliette and I get back?"

He raised his brows.

"From Queenstown," she explained. "We'll probably be back Wednesday."

"I'm trying to set up a meeting in Sydney for the end of the week."

Ethan fancied she looked a little downcast. Something compelled him to start negotiating. "Even if I do have to go before you get back, they're only meetings. And meetings don't take forever."

"And the flight's only a few hours," she encouraged him.

"Exactly." Ethan leaned forward and rested his elbow on the barrel. "You might think," he said slowly, "that takes the pressure off."

Lucy nodded, looking relieved.

Until he reached for her hand and sandwiched it between both of his. Her eyes flew wide and he stroked firmly over the base of her thumb to confirm the scramble of her pulse.

The girl with her boyfriend's knee wedged between her thighs gave a low breathless moan. It hung between them, and they stared at each other, connected by the lingering memory of the moan and the thumping of her pulse under his thumb.

"However," he murmured, "I don't think you should be too complacent."

Tom picked her up early the next day in one of the lodge's vehicles, anxious to be on the road. It was safari day for the hunters, and the day Lucy and Juliette were to leave for Queenstown. On the way to the Australians' hotel, she advised Tom to report the stolen car, regardless of the registration issue. He seemed vague about Joseph Dunn, which perplexed her. "Whatever." She shrugged. "Probably just kids. It just seemed strange he actually mentioned seeing your car."

They arrived back at Summerhill and organized their day. The four hunters, Tom, Stacey the tracker, Magnus and an Indonesian guest, departed. Lucy and Juliette packed and she arranged for Ellie to drop them at the airstrip. Summerhill had its own airstrip. A good proportion of the guests chartered light aircraft for hunting or excursions. The women would first be flown to Aorangi, Australasia's highest mountain, and then to Queenstown, a popular tourist mecca in the south.

Lucy had put her luggage in the car boot and was walking down the hallway when a hand snaked out of the alcove going into Tom's office. Suddenly she was hauled up against a wall of warm skin, taut muscle and bone.

"Not thinking of leaving without saying goodbye?"

"Ethan!" Her heart thumped against her ribs. For one awful moment, Joseph Dunn's face had flashed through her mind. "What are you…?"

"Told you not to be complacent."

She relaxed slightly, her eyes adjusting to the gloom with the aid of the gleam of his teeth.

One slick maneuver and she found herself turned, her back against the wall—or at least the wall-mounted firearms cabinet. His teeth flashed again. "Wow. Nice suit. But I'd love to see you in red."

Lucy felt herself flush. As was her way, she was taking her client's lead. Juliette favored short skirts, in vibrant reds and pinks. Lucy's choice was a dusky-pink color with a barely-there skirt and high black pumps. The lacy black cami under the jacket touched it off nicely even though she would be no match for the beauty and wealth of Mrs. Anderson.

"The guys in Queenstown won't know what hit them when you two roll into town."

His hands snaked around her waist, inside the jacket. "Ethan, I thought we agreed last night…"

"…that we had a mutual attraction." He leaned back, smiling and swaying her gently.

"That nothing was going to…" She couldn't help it, she was smiling back.

"…happen last night," he finished.

She shook her head. "Ha, ha. I have to go. The plane's waiting."

"She can afford a few more minutes." He leaned in close, eyes slanted down to her mouth. His thighs brushed hers. Lucy's breath hissed through her lips as warmth flooded her agitated body. When she felt herself about to sag against him, she put a restraining hand on his chest and leaned her head back.

An unexpected jerk and a sharp click behind her head claimed Ethan's attention.

He frowned. "Bit lax isn't it? The firearms cabinet left unlocked?"

Lucy was still concentrating on his mouth, centimeters away. "Tom must have forgotten," she said dreamily.

The stern, all-business look he gave her snapped her out of her fog.

"Tom forget often?"

"No, I don't think so."

This was bad. This was a serious issue, one that could have their firearms license revoked. New Zealand's firearms laws were strictly enforced. This could impinge on staying in the club. "I'll get the key."

Ethan fingered the cabinet's latch. "It's not good enough, Lucy. Anyone could have access."

Lucy did the only possible thing she could think of. She reached up to tangle her fingers in his thick hair and pulled his head down to hers.

His hair was soft, inviting her to twist and tug gently. She felt his hand, still around her waist, spread and lift and next thing she was on tiptoe, planted against the length of him like ivy. He held back slightly, his brow still furrowed in a frown. His free hand moved up to the back of her head and his fingers mirrored what hers were doing.

She tugged him closer and he sank into her mouth. Hot and humid, his satiny-slick tongue danced with hers. Lucy wound her hands around his neck and pressed her tingling nipples into him. She fought to breathe; he took all her air and gave it back in miserly doses and she heard his breath rasping through his nostrils.

His strength surprised her. The tension in his neck, each and every finger spread wide on her back, the muscles in his thighs pressed up against hers—it was all leashed power.

Her mind shut down. She didn't care about the key or the cabinet. She didn't worry that someone would walk down the hallway and see them. Professionalism was as far from her mind as Africa. Her blood was roaring. She wanted him unleashed.

Lucy moaned, a sound of impatience that sounded like "more." She caged his face with both hands and kissed as she'd dreamed of doing the last few days, since that first long look. His body was firm all over. In one place, cast iron. But all that flashed in her agitated mind. It was his mouth she wanted, his earthy, erotic flavor that went straight to her head like champagne, sweeping all obstacles aside.

Ethan pulled away first. That embarrassed her, though it took a moment or two to understand. She looked at his throat, gulping in some much-needed air. When she dredged up the nerve to look at his face, his pale-blue eyes simmered. He carefully exhaled.

"Oh, boy," he said softly. "You have my undivided attention."

"I'd better go," she whispered back.

Ethan took a reluctant step back and she weaved around him and started to walk, hoping her knees would hold her until she got out of his sight. She made it ten feet before her name clipped her to a halt. Turning reluctantly back because she just *knew* she'd be the color of mortified beetroot, she focused again on the golden skin of his throat.

"The key?" He jabbed his thumb toward the cabinet. Lucy nodded at him stupidly. "Silly me."

She walked unsteadily toward him, veered left into Tom's office and found the key in the top drawer. All the while, his eyes burned into her. He took the key, locked the cabinet then dropped it back into her palm.

"Key should be locked away also," he told her gently.

"Okay." She proceeded to replace the key right where she'd found it and walked out past him, still with the stupid half smile on her face. "See ya," she murmured dazedly, and escaped up the stairs.

Six

Lucy happily escaped the crowds at the gondola and chose a much quieter observation point, only a couple of hundred meters from the township. The view might not be as spectacular but pretty landscapes were not lacking in her life. Summerhill was her magic place.

She fished in her purse for coins to operate the shiny telescope, new since her last visit.

Bored, bored, bored. Poor Juliette had barely been out of her room since they had arrived, having succumbed to some sort of tummy bug. They'd had such a nice time the first day, flying over Aorangi, then jet-boating on the lake when they got to Queenstown, and a nice dinner last night. Then Juliette canceled breakfast and it all went downhill from there. Her illness set in and Lucy was left to amuse herself.

A noisy family group ascended the lookout platform and two or three young children scampered about. Lucy panned the township and easily picked out her hotel, the largest in Queenstown and right on the waterfront. Her room on the fourth floor boasted views over the supermarket parking lot. Juliette had the ninth floor Presidential Suite, and a presidential balcony to go with it.

And there she was! Lucy grinned in childish elation. Juliette stood on her balcony, wearing *that* robe. The filmy deep purple number Lucy had admired last night. The robe that would look average on anyone else but Juliette with her statuesque figure.

She was distracted by the determined gaze of the youngest of the family group who fixed her with a come-on-lady! look. When she beaded in on Juliette again, she realized her friend wasn't alone. It was difficult to discern expression—she fiddled with the focus dial—but Juliette appeared to be shaking her head and her mouth was open.

Then a cocoa-dark head moved into view and Lucy's stomach lurched. His back was turned, but she would know that haughty bearing, those broad shoulders anywhere. He was jacketless and his shirtsleeves were rolled up midway to his elbows.

Lucy stepped back, her lips moving soundlessly as questions reared up like hands in a classroom.

"Mum, I want a go!" the small boy yelled. Lucy ignored him and moved forward again.

Ethan and Juliette. In her suite. Midday in Queenstown, hundreds of kilometers from where he was meant to be. When Juliette was supposed to be ill and had insisted Lucy follow the schedule they had planned.

With Juliette in *that* robe.

Suddenly Juliette swirled around and made for the

balcony door. Ethan grabbed her arm, holding her just above the elbow. They stood for some moments like that and again Lucy could not focus quite well enough to say for sure what the woman's emotions were.

But one thing was as obvious as a train wreck. These two people had a lot more going on than they had disclosed.

The little boy sighed loudly. Lucy glanced at him and pulled a scowling face. His eyes widened, but he didn't say anything.

Over on the balcony, Juliette had tugged her arm away and disappeared into the suite. Lucy watched Ethan hesitate for a second or two and run his hands through his hair. Then he moved inside with a determined stride, closing the glass door behind him. Lucy squinted but the reflection off the glass prevented her seeing inside the suite.

Her head lifted above the telescope. She stared out into space, a million questions pelting her, until a polite cough behind her made her turn. "Oh." She looked at the entire family line-up in a daze. "Sorry."

"That's all right, dear," the woman said kindly. "Is it a nice view?"

Lucy stepped off the platform. The impatient child scampered up and took her place, and Lucy just nodded and walked away.

"Foreigner, I think," she heard the woman comment.

As she began the walk down, she attempted to find a plausible explanation. They wouldn't. They were not cheats. She refused to believe she could be so wrong about people.

He'd come with a message from Magnus. He was bored and looking for Lucy. It wasn't him. She could not be one hundred percent sure…

Disappointment turned her mouth down. Of course that was Ethan. No one could emulate those endless legs, that eat-up-the-miles gait as he'd followed Juliette inside.

That made a lie of his assertion that he'd never met Magnus's wife before his arrival at Summerhill. She had been right beside them at their odd, tension-filled introduction. Then there were the loaded looks he shot Juliette when he thought no one was watching. Lucy thought it was because of his disdain for wealthy women, especially after hearing the story of his childhood. It would be strange if he weren't carrying around some residual prejudice.

A couple of anguished hours later, she knocked on Juliette's door. That took a lot of courage. If he'd been there, Lucy had no idea what she would have said. But he wasn't—unless he was hiding in the shower. And Juliette was still pale and subdued.

"Have you been out?" Lucy's voice caught in her throat as she walked into the suite and saw through to the rumpled bed. *Stop.*

"No," Juliette said.

"Did you get the doctor?"

"No. I'm feeling a little better."

"Poor you," Lucy mumbled. "You must have been bored silly today." Her eyes searched Juliette's face.

"I just read." The woman shrugged.

Lucy left to arrange the charter flight that would leave half a day earlier than they had planned. Her feet dragged. It was true. If it had been an innocent visit, Juliette would have mentioned it.

They were lovers. Liars. Betraying Magnus.

Oh, they made a handsome couple. Juliette was exactly the sort of woman she would expect Ethan to have on his arm—lovely, sophisticated, worldly. He wouldn't seriously be interested in an undersized airhead like her. No brains to save her. No qualifications. Poverty grinning over her threshold.

Oh, he didn't know that. That was the whole point…

But he seemed to like her. His eyes told her he liked her very much. His mouth told her he was hungry for hers. He didn't even seem to mind that she walked around with her big, fat foot in her mouth all day.

Lucy's chest tightened. How could someone you barely knew have the power to hurt you this much?

He wouldn't take her in again. She did not mind being thought of as an easy touch, but she was damned if she would let that man kindle hope in her again. She was nothing but a diversion. A subterfuge. It was Juliette he wanted.

The morning flight back to Summerhill was a quiet affair. Juliette still claimed to feel awful. Lucy's suspicions and hurt had ballooned overnight but she did not broach the subject. She was torn. She wanted to know—*how* she wanted to know. But one word from Juliette could make or break Summerhill in Magnus's eyes. Lucy could not afford to alienate her.

They arrived back at Summerhill in the early afternoon, much more restrained than before. Lucy jumped out and hefted Juliette's classy luggage and vanity from the boot.

Ellie welcomed them back. "Let me," she ordered.

Lucy normally wouldn't dream of letting the older woman carry luggage upstairs, but Summerhill wasn't her comforting refuge today. She had no wish to run into Ethan while she felt so raw.

Citing an appointment, she bade them a brisk goodbye and roared off into town.

* * *

It was the morning from hell.

At ten-thirty, Summerhill's former meat supplier from the village turned up at her apartment, saying he had already been to the lodge looking for Tom. It transpired that he had instigated proceedings against Summerhill for unpaid accounts. Tom was to have responded to the civil court claim to pay the arrears within thirty days or dispute the claim. Time was up. The civil court, in the absence of any action by the lodge to respond, had made judgment in favor of Hogan's Meats.

Lucy was stunned. It was the first she had heard of it. She and Tom had known the Hogans all their lives. Mr. Hogan told her that Summerhill owed several thousand to the family-owned business, which had been chasing them up for over a year.

Mr. Hogan warned her that if full payment was not received within a month, he would make application to put Summerhill Lodge Holdings into liquidation. In that event, he said, he would be at the front of a very long queue.

She sat at her desk with the official documents in her hand and Mr. Hogan sitting across from her. Staring blindly at the papers, she apologized again and again and promised to make Tom write the check the moment he returned from the hunt.

Then Mr. Hogan passed a comment that stopped her in her tracks.

"I'm talking now as an old friend of your father's. Well, used to be. There are a lot of people getting pretty tired of dealing with Summerhill. You'd better shape up. Someone's sniffing around. People don't know if it's the Inland Revenue Department or a liquidator. Hell, could be a private investigator. I personally wish you no harm, at least I won't once I get my money. But there are others who would gladly blab. Missed payments, wages held back, bad debts. Watch your back is what I'm saying."

After he'd gone, Lucy succumbed to a teeth-clenching tension headache, accompanied by a fit of self-indulgent crying. God, she was so stupid, so naive to think she could help run this business. Everyone would be so much better off without her.

Foreboding prickled at the back of her neck. There was something going on here that she had no comprehension of, and Tom obviously found her too lacking in business sense to share his problems.

Why had she come back? She had never been wanted here. What was different? So much easier to run away, as she always had when their indifference rankled.

The doorbell rang again. Now what? She hurriedly blew her nose and wiped her face on the way to the door. Ethan Rae, looking dangerously alert for the hour, strolled into the hallway. "Morning."

Too surprised to protest, she took a step back and he walked past her. Closing her eyes, her body sank back against the wall for a few fortifying seconds. This was just what she needed. She pushed herself away from the wall. "What can I…" Hurrying after him, she almost ran into the solid wall of his back, finding he'd stopped to let her catch up. She dug her toes into the floor and suppressed a sigh of frustration. "Do for you?"

Ethan stepped back against the wall and motioned her past. "*This* is where you live."

She led the way into her little office. He followed at his own pace, giving her living room an interested study.

"Is that a McCahon?" He gestured to a painting in the dining area by a well-known New Zealand artist whose works spanned the fifties through to the eighties. "That must be quite valuable."

"A twenty-first-birthday present from my father," she told him. Her father had used money as a way to keep distance. Like this apartment he'd bought for her when she was barely out of school—it had kept her away from Summerhill and out of his hair.

Lucy sat at her desk, turning the legal documents facedown. It was so unfair. After the morning she'd just endured and before she could compose herself, Ethan was the very last person she wanted to see.

He did not budge when she indicated the chair behind him, just stood looking down at her intently. Could he see how upset and tense she was? It was her curse to have a damn face that showed everything. She dragged on all her reserves in a massive effort to relax.

He looked so good, still in snappy black pants but a more casual butter-colored shirt that did wonderful things for his eyes. It was hard to recall what she was angry with him for.

"Can I help you with something?" She focused on a spot over his shoulder.

"Spend the day with me." No hesitation. Just like that.

Her eyes skidded to his and astonishment pushed her voice up high. "What?"

"It's what you do, isn't it? Entertain clients?"

"Um—today?" Her voice sounded thready.

His eyes narrowed with something like concern. "Yes, today. What's wrong, Lucy?"

If he starts being nice to me, I'll burst into tears, she thought frenziedly. Forget this morning, and *be careful*. She must not let on about the morning's events. She cleared her throat, seeking a firmer tone. "I can't today. You should have given me some warning."

He perched on the edge of her desk and she tried not to be riveted by the pull of expensive black fabric stretched across long thighs.

"What are you doing?"

"What?" she squeaked, dragging her eyes back to his face.

"Today. Meetings? Clients to keep waiting at the airport? Lovely trophy wives to entertain?"

That comment jabbed her right in the heart. He had been the one entertaining a lovely trophy wife. Should she casually ask, "By the way, how long have you and Juliette been lovers?"

Lucy took a deep breath, wishing him away. Wishing her brain would unscramble enough for her to give him a professional and firm negative. Above all else, she couldn't afford to show her distress. If he knew of the financial problems besetting Summerhill, Magnus would hear of it and Tom would go ape.

She kept her eyes down, ineffectually moving things around on her desk and mangling the tissue in her hands into a mess of tufts.

But her heart leapt into her throat when his index finger landed under her chin, tilting it up.

"You've been crying." His voice was gentle. It nearly did her in completely when he pulled another tissue from the box and handed it to her.

Ethan sensed the moment he walked in that she was upset, shaken even. Why that should concern him, he had no idea, yet it did. He wasn't even sure why he was here, except that he'd utilized his time well in the last couple of days and felt he deserved a break. He'd spent hours preparing for the Turtle Island meetings. Made a few inquiries around the region regarding Summerhill.

Today he had come straight from the Seabrook MacKenzie Dyslexia Center in town and had a pocketful of leaflets, but stayed his hand from reaching for them.

He was looking forward to some more of the easy, flirting banter they seemed to draw from each other. Maybe looking forward to another delicious kiss.

Okay, maybe hoping for a lot more than that.

But something was badly wrong. She looked beaten. Forgetting the brochures, he pulled a tissue from the box on her desk and handed it to her.

She took the tissue he offered and disposed of the remains of the one in her hand. "No I haven't."

She was lying. Her eyelashes were wet. He marveled at the surge of testosterone that rolled through him. Ever since he'd met Lucy McKinlay, he'd been walking around baring his teeth and beating his chest. Trying to impress her in the pool. Wanting to rip that guy's face off at the game.

"Who's upset you? Is it Tom?" The harshness of his voice grated. Now he was ready to take on her brother. What was the matter with him?

Lucy shook her head, moving pads and pens, a stapler from one place to another on her desk. Anything to avoid looking right at him. "Tom's away, remember?"

She sniffed loudly. There was a slightly sullen plumpness to her lips and her back was ramrod straight.

Ethan got up off the desk, pulled the chair up and sat with his elbows on her desk. "I'm not leaving until you tell me what's wrong." He leaned forward and down so their faces were on the same level.

Lucy shook her head stubbornly. For a brief second, he considered leaving her to her mood. He had work to do. He needed to stay focused, not run around mopping up tears.

But right now, she wasn't talking.

He sighed. "Okay, Lucy, show me how upset you're *not* by coming out with me."

Then her features changed subtly, as if she had made a decision. She stood and moved around the desk. By the time she got to him and looked down on him, the sullenness had fallen away. Her eyes lit up the room with sunshine. A saucy little smile whispered of an intimacy he could only dream of.

"You're right. It's a beautiful winter's day. Let's not waste it indoors."

She hadn't put out her hand but he felt a sweet glow of warmth as if she had touched him. Something worrisome nagged at him.

But he pushed it away. He was happy to be here. He could tell himself all day that he was doing his job, checking out Summerhill for Magnus. But in truth, he couldn't stay away.

Lucy chattered on brightly, grabbing her coat, telling him she would drive, gathering up a handful of brochures to look at. The chattering continued as she dashed confidently around the streets in her little car. She allowed him the odd grunt or nod to the questions she asked, but for the most part, he sat quietly, wondering what she was hiding.

His inquiries in the village had turned up quite a bit to be concerned about. Tom was in it right up to his neck and Ethan bet that Lucy had little idea of what was going on. From what he'd heard, things were accelerating and it was only a matter of time until the other shoe dropped.

And this burst of bright activity and energy—he realized Lucy was trying to distract him. Just like the other day at the firearms cabinet when she had kissed him to distract him, to conceal something, to cover up for her brother.

What had she said? She was naughty at school to cover up her dyslexia. The more he thought about it, the more he was sure she used her charm to cover up a deep sense of powerlessness at what was happening in her life.

Seven

"Talk a lot, don't you?" he injected in a rare pause.

She compressed her lips in a rueful grin. "Have you only just noticed?"

Ethan chuckled and stretched, glad to be here with her. He was too big for this tiny sports car, which only served to remind him of her proximity and the scent he missed when she wasn't around.

He could be distracted. Lust rippled over his nerve endings and he sighed in pleasure. Lust he could handle.

"I'm glad you invited me out," he told her.

"Really?" The word turned down at the end, telling him dyslexic she may be, but she recognized tongue-in-cheek when she heard it. "What did you have in mind?"

"You're the tour guide. Make a plan."

Whatever was worrying her, she'd obviously decided to put it behind her. "That's right. There has to be a plan."

"Uh-huh."

"Do you ever do anything just for the hell of it?"

Ethan thought for a few seconds. "Once, on a mountain, I kissed a girl after knowing her only a few hours."

Lucy glanced at him briefly. He caught a flash of that flirty look she got sometimes, right before she remembered she was trying to keep it professional.

Then she grinned. "Truly heroic."

They drove through a long tunnel and into a small harbor town about twenty minutes from the city center. A visiting cruise ship dominated the berthed container ships and fishing vessels.

"I heard this ship was in town. How about a cruise tour?"

The *Princess Athena* was one of the largest liners in the world. Three hundred meters long, sixteen stories high, and solid-gold luxury.

The passengers were off sightseeing or shopping in Christchurch. Parts of the ship were on display to interested sightseers, though the security guards nearly outnumbered the visitors.

Lucy dragged him from bars to ballrooms to casinos to beauty salons and boutique shops. Afterwards they tossed a coin for choice of food and ended up eating fish and chips out of paper on a low wall along one of the lesser wharfs. They watched kids fishing off the wharf, bundled up in brightly colored anoraks. The sea chopped up into agitated whitecaps and seagulls screeched and strutted around them.

"I am seriously going to have to find myself a rich husband, and fast," Lucy commented, her eyes on the *Princess Athena*.

Ethan had been munching on a satisfyingly salty

piece of fish which suddenly turned to paste in his mouth. He wished she hadn't said that.

"I defy you to find me one woman," she continued, "barring the criminally insane, who would turn down a cruise on a baby like that."

An excited cry from the clutch of children distracted her. "Oh look, they've caught something."

Ethan flung the piece of food into the air. Seagulls rose up and then down to scramble for their prize.

But when she turned back to him, her face was so open and animated, no trace of the shadows of the morning. He told himself it was a throwaway remark.

Anyway, at this point, they were sharing a friendly day out. Nothing more complicated than that.

"Tell me about your job," Lucy demanded, choosing a fat chip, bending her head back to lower it into her mouth.

Ethan explained his role in Magnus's corporation. Scouting tourist resort locations, negotiating the deal, organizing architects and surveyors and necessary permits. "Everything from bribery to schmoozing with local councils, religious leaders and politicians."

Once the consents were secured, he would hire and supervise building crews, interior designers and tradespeople for the finishing. The management and staff came last. "I generally stay around for the first month or so of operation," he explained. "One project can take up to two years."

He told her about Turtle Island, his father and Magnus's history with the island, and how once it was completed—provided he got the deal—it would be his last.

"What then?"

"I don't know. Some piece of farm land somewhere."

"You want to farm?" she asked curiously. "I'd have

thought you would shy away from that, after your childhood."

"Part of me wants to prove I can do it, I suppose," he said thoughtfully. "Prove I can make a better job of it this time round."

"Prove you are a better farmer than your father, you mean."

Ethan chuckled. "That wouldn't be hard." He lifted his bottled water and took a swig. "Enough about me. Did you always want to look after trophy wives?"

Lucy laughed and wiped her fingers on a tissue. "Being dyslexic kind of stifles any great ambition. I've never really thought in terms of a long-lasting career. But there are a few things I'd like to do to improve Summerhill."

"Such as?" he asked, interested.

Lucy shrugged. "They'll never come to anything. Tom doesn't think I have a lot to offer."

Remembering the brochures, he wiped his hands and drew them from his jacket pocket. "I went to the Seabrook MacKenzie Dyslexia center this morning."

She took the brochures, a little line between her brows as she perused them quickly.

"Have you ever had an assessment, Lucy?"

She shook her head. "They once arranged an appointment for me at school." She shrugged carelessly. "Must've been busy that day."

"People with learning disabilities have different strengths and weaknesses. They learn to enhance their strengths to compensate." He tapped the brochures she still held. "Without an assessment, you won't know what your strengths are. It wouldn't take long, Lucy. Half a day."

Another rise of her shoulders. "Tom does the office stuff. I spent ages memorizing all the brochures and tourist stuff so I don't really need to be able to read. I mean, I *can* read, just not quickly and it's hard with other people about."

"I think you're selling yourself short."

"Just be glad you're not my boss," she quipped. "How come you know so much about it?"

"Dyslexia is something Magnus cares a lot about—he's dyslexic himself. He's made sure his workforce is well-supported. Do you know, one in ten people have a learning difficulty?"

Lucy grinned. "We're sneaking around all over the place."

Ethan guessed she was so accustomed to sweeping her problems under the carpet, she probably did not even notice she was being flippant. He pushed the brochures toward her. He was a patient man.

"Tell me about your plans for Summerhill."

"Ideas, not plans," she corrected him. "Plans have to be written down."

"Okay." He took a small notebook and pen from his jacket's inside pocket. "You tell me the ideas, I write them down and get my secretary to type them up." He looked at her, his pen poised over the notebook.

Lucy gulped. "That's nice of you, but they're not ready to be drawn up into a business plan. They're just some thoughts…"

"What thoughts, Lucy?"

She wiped her mouth and hands and picked up the remnants of the cooling food, dumping it onto the ground a few feet away. With enough racket to wake the dead, the seagulls closed in and Lucy dropped the empty paper into a bin close by.

She sat back down hesitantly, obviously afraid he would laugh at her ideas. He convinced her otherwise.

She had some great ideas, and he told her so. Courtesy vans for the village restaurants. Targeted advertising to golf clubs because of the world class Terrace Downs golf course that had been completed nearby recently. A health and beauty spa for the guests, including massage, hair salon, facials and a gym. Using Summerhill as a conference and function center. Tom could still have his hunting safaris but they could also offer weddings, whodunit nights, workshops…the list was endless.

Ethan was impressed. He wrote everything down, cautioning against one or two things, just from a financial perspective. But most of her ideas were very viable, relevant to her market, and wouldn't cost too much in initial outlay.

"And then I could spend some time on the farm. Tom doesn't have time these days—he's more interested in the lodge. Since the farm manager quit, things have gotten out of hand. I'd love to see it back to full production."

Ethan had noticed the farm's neglect on his rides. It was very understocked, the pastures in poor condition.

They talked till the wind rose and chased the sun and the children away. Lucy lapped up his praise of her ideas as if she had never received a compliment in all her life.

"You are as sharp as a tack, Lucy," he told her, "and don't you let anyone tell you any different."

She glowed, a stranger to approbation. A late bloomer, and it occurred to him he'd like to nurture that and watch it grow. Without her brother pushing her down all the time, there were no limits to what she could achieve with a little encouragement.

And then he remembered Turtle Island. If Magna-

Corp successfully negotiated the deal, there would be no way he could spare the time to enjoy watching her grow.

How far was New Zealand from the islands, anyway?

Lucy uncapped a bottle of water and drank deeply, bending her head back and exposing the milky skin of her throat. A substantial urge to kiss her steamrolled him so completely, he held his breath for an age, worried there wouldn't be another. She was so fresh, with a natural, almost childlike beauty. Her eyes showed every emotion.

She brought the bottle away and licked her lips, then raised her eyes to his. Ethan was a second or two behind, his eyes still devouring the sight of the tip of her pink tongue slipping between her lips and trapping a bead of moisture at one corner. He mimicked her, an involuntary action, his own tongue darting out and touching his mouth. This close, he could see traces of the beige-pink-tinted lip gloss she applied regularly.

He saw his thoughts, his desire leap in her eyes. Some magnetic force seemed to drag them toward each other, eyes locked, oblivious to their surroundings. The pull was palpable in the diminishing distance.

She broke the impasse when he lifted his hand, intending to cup her face and draw her to him. The desire on her face was extinguished in one blink. Then it was all motion and half sentences: "Well, we'd better…" She scooped up their water bottles. "Look at the time." Slapping pockets for keys. "Got everything?" Hustling him toward the car.

When they reached the car, Ethan grabbed her hand and tugged gently until they leaned on the passenger door, side by side. He absently twisted the chunky white-gold channel ring that emphasized her delicate bones, and tried to absorb, to understand the all-consuming desire he had for her.

Never had he let his desires rule him. Always, he played the seduction game without losing sight of who he was, why he was there, where this was going—or not, usually. Right at this moment, the *Titanic* could be sinking and he wouldn't budge an inch if she were in his arms. Damn fool. He was so consumed by want, it didn't even frighten him.

He laced his fingers through hers, studied her small white hand, short neat nails painted with a clear gloss. He traced the visible bluish veins under the skin, wanted to be that life force for her.

There was no telling where this preoccupation would lead, but he was fast coming to the conclusion it was a necessary journey.

But then Lucy trembled and tugged to free her hand, accompanied by a small huff of agitation. He watched her chin rise in defiance and her small tense body brace.

"What?"

"Why bother flirting with me when we both know it's Juliette you want?" Her eyes were dark with disappointment, her voice cool.

He hadn't seen that coming and was jolted right out of desire and swimming in confusion. "Where the hell did that come from?"

"I saw you in Queenstown. On her balcony."

Realization dawned. He raised his hands to his head, rested them there. There was no easy way out of this. "Did you ask her about it?"

Lucy hesitated. "Let's say I gave her the opportunity to tell me you were there." Her mouth turned down miserably. "She didn't take it."

Ethan considered his options. He hadn't gained a

thing in the trip to Queenstown. Juliette was so in-
censed, she had virtually thrown him out of her hotel
suite. But last night at Summerhill after he'd shown her
the newspaper clippings he'd been sent, she calmed
enough to talk to him.

"Lucy, I have no romantic interest in Juliette." He
said it quietly and tried to convey sincerity, for it was
the truth.

She raised her chin, one brow arched high, her eyes
direct and challenging.

He sighed. "I had some concerns about her reasons
for marrying Magnus."

He'd spent an hour on the phone to the investigator
yesterday. Forensics had concluded a silencer had been
used, which explained Juliette's claim she had not heard
the shot and had slept the night, discovering her husband's body on deck the next morning. There were actually several witnesses, not just the one reported by the
papers, who had seen a strange yacht in the vicinity. Yet,
that vessel had disappeared off the face of the earth.

Ethan rubbed a hand over his face. She had made a
new life for herself after two years of hateful media intrusion and innuendo. If the Australian press got wind
of the story, her nightmare would begin all over again.
And that would be devastating, for her and for a well-
respected and successful businessman.

Juliette had sworn him to secrecy until she could
talk to Magnus about it. He inhaled deeply, looking
into Lucy's eyes. "I'm going to have to ask you to trust
me on this. For now."

Lucy slumped a little. The defiance seemed to tick
slowly over into acceptance as he watched, but it was a
bitter sort of acceptance. The shadows from this morning had returned.

"Trust you, hey?" Her mouth curved in a small smile that did not reach her eyes. And then she shrugged and turned away.

While he battled with his conscience, Lucy walked around to the driver's door, yanking it open. Before she got in, she looked haughtily across the roof of the car. "Doesn't matter to me. I'm just a professional companion, remember? And—" she raised her arm and checked her watch "—I'll be on overtime if I don't get you back to your car soon."

Ethan flinched as the door slammed shut.

She got behind the wheel, fuming with indignation. For a few minutes today, she'd been on the trip of a lifetime. She had basked in the glow of his praise. For a few minutes, she'd felt that he liked her for herself. Found her funny and charming, saw past the dyslexia. He had listened, encouraged, offered to help.

And man, he was the sexiest thing on legs. Every single feature, every aspect of him seemed to pull her toward him, draw her in until she wanted to be absorbed by him. One smoldering look—and with his deeply tanned skin, dark hair and those glorious pale eyes, he smoldered like embers ever threatening to ignite into a bush fire.

But she needed to clear up the Juliette thing.

When he balked at telling her the full story, she was plunged back into cold familiar waters. Silly little Lucy. Gullible, aching for affection and attention. She'd believe anything.

Oh, she knew he wanted her. Even the most sophisticated and experienced seducer could not fake the desire she'd glimpsed. But he did not think enough of her to tell the truth. He'd expected mindless response to his praise and pretence at caring. God help her, he'd very nearly gotten it!

He wanted her to trust him? He would have to work harder than that.

Ethan opened the passenger door and climbed in. His movements were slow and deliberate, and although she did her level best not to look at him, the waves of frustration sloughed off him and settled over her.

Her indignation cooled a little. Remember what's at stake here. She may already have endangered Summerhill by accusing him of having an affair with his boss's wife. Having him sulk for the rest of the day was not a good idea. She was supposed to be helping him enjoy his stay.

Tension sizzled. She breathed it in. "I'm sorry," she said, not intending it to sound so tight.

"What do you have to be sorry about?"

"I've upset you."

His lips pursed. "Hmm. Upset?" His legs stretched out in a taut line and he rested his hands on his thighs. "Well now. Horny? Very. Confused? Worried that your brother is taking advantage of you?"

He paused and flexed his fingers.

Lucy's mind skittered away from all but the safest word. "Confused?"

He grunted. "I don't need this, Lucy. I've got stuff to do."

"Don't let me stop you," she responded tartly.

"But you do, and that's the rub. Even when I'm not with you, I'm thinking about you and worrying about you, and dreaming of that damn mouth of yours."

Said mouth dropped open, but all she could manage was "Oh." There wasn't really a lot you could say to that.

With his deep slow drawl still echoing in her ears,

she felt herself blush. There was nothing she could do about that either. She kept her eyes firmly on the road ahead and that was the last they spoke.

But her body and mind spoke—plenty. She was so aware of every movement, every breath he took. For the most part he stared straight ahead. But now and again she felt a wave of heat as he glanced over at her. Lucy did not return his glances but steamed away in her own humid shell.

She felt she was clinging to a cloud and any minute her weight would drag her through it. The longer and more tense the silence, the more heavy-limbed and languorous she felt. His breathing sounded loud in her ears—but maybe it was her own. She changed gears, navigated, all on autopilot, while struggling with equal measures of worry and desire and self-righteousness. If she couldn't tamp it down, she thought she might explode.

All of a sudden they were in the underground garage at her building and she was turning off the ignition. Before she had time to wonder why she hadn't dropped him at his rental car across the road, he made his move. She heard the click of his seatbelt release almost just before she felt her own released. Without a word, his hands gripped her shoulders, turning her quickly, then moving down to clamp around her waist and lift her right up out of her seat. Her hands flailed for balance and a surprised shriek raced out of her throat. "What—?"

Next moment, she was hoisted over the handbrake and plonked ungraciously and haphazardly onto his lap, bumping her head on the ceiling of the car. Quick as a flash, one hand clasped the back of her neck and her head was pulled down, close to his face.

Lucy suddenly remembered to breathe and exhaled

raggedly. Ethan's eyes were open and they flashed bright with anger. He held her head fast, millimeters away. His hot breath huffed across her face and his fingers laced through her hair. "It's *you* I want, not Juliette," he growled. "And to hell with your professionalism!"

Then his mouth claimed hers and Lucy was lost. His lips forced hers open. Teeth scraped and ground together. His tongue burst into her mouth, demanding her response, not her permission. This was no magical fairy-tale kiss on a mountain, with Mother Nature smiling benevolently down. Nor a stolen smooch in an alcove that she had initiated. This was hard, carnal. As if he was staking a claim.

And after the tensions of the day, it mirrored her feelings exactly.

As her initial shock subsided, Lucy was taken over by the heat of his body, the pressure of his mouth. Her taut muscles relaxed, sank into him as he deepened the kiss. Her hands were trapped between them and she struggled vaguely to free them but his chest was unyielding, his arms like iron. One hand moved, uncurled so the palm was flat against his chest. The other remained fisted with his shirt locked into it, only now she pulled him closer.

Perhaps realizing Lucy was past struggling, Ethan's hand at the back of her head gentled. Straightening his fingers, he stroked and tugged at her hair. She shivered, every nerve ending rising to the surface.

His tongue also gentled. Instead of insistence, there was now an erotic rhythm that had her squirming even closer. Their tongues met, slid over each other and back again, and she felt the different textures of his, and his gentle but insistent probing. Her breath started to labor in serious excitement.

He made her feel things she'd never experienced. How could she resist the pull of her body when it responded to him so frenetically? When this ended, when he was gone, would she ever feel desire again?

Her head fell back slightly and she gasped as he moved his mouth down her throat then along her jawline to end with a hot lick and suck at the base of her ear. She arched her back, surging against him. His hand left her head and joined the other in a firm caress down the length of her sides, and soon she felt them inside her knit top.

As they strained against each other, she heard a moan of impatience—hers. They writhed and pressed. She rubbed her bottom down into his lap, seeking, finding the hard ridge that strained up to meet her, and heard his grunt, desperate and loud in the confined space. Lucy squirmed in his lap, trying to crawl in as close as she could get.

His hands spanned her waist and were then inching up toward her breasts. A slave to sensation at this point, Lucy shamelessly dipped her body down, craving the exquisite torment when his thumbs grazed over her aching nipples. The blood roared in her ears. So far, so fast, she couldn't believe she was this close. One more thrust of his tongue, one more squeeze of her nipples to send a flame of pure lust licking downward, one more mighty flex of his thighs to push and grind him into the most sensitive part of her. She was seconds away, the scream already tearing up toward her throat.

And then he tore his mouth from hers, his chest rising against her. His hands stilled their torture. She opened her eyes, moaning with impatience. Their breath mingled, hot and humid. He looked up into her eyes and said, "Your call."

"Upstairs, now!" Lucy gasped.

She scrambled back over to her side of the car, haphazardly pulling down her top. Grabbing the keys from the ignition, she opened the door, fumbled for her bag, and rounded the car, intent only on getting upstairs.

Ethan was alighting from the passenger side. She hesitated impatiently, her pulse hammering in her throat. Hurry, hurry, she chanted mentally, the fingers of one hand pressing on the spot in her chest where the blood pounded and rushed. When she knew Ethan was right behind her, she turned toward the stairs and ran—smack!—into a stranger.

Eight

The man put out a steadying hand from where he leaned against the wall of the underground garage. Lucy backed away as if he held a whip.

She could only imagine her dishevelled appearance, but his eyes were on Ethan, who drew alongside her. Then he looked back at her shame-burned face. "Lucy McKinlay, I presume?"

"How—how do you know?"

He indicated the number of her parking spot. The number of her apartment.

His eyes slid back to her. With a smug little look on his face, he introduced himself as a detective.

Ethan moved closer, tidying his shirt. His arms dropped to his sides. One of them brushed against hers and he deliberately stepped slightly in front, shielding her.

The only thought Lucy could put together was that

she was as bad as her mother. She didn't suppose he was there to arrest them for lewd public behavior, but still, to know he'd seen them in the car, practically like animals... Shame, shame, so hot, she could die of it.

Ethan exhaled. "What's the problem, detective?"

"And you are, sir?"

"Ethan Rae. I'm a friend."

The detective gave another smug little smile then got down to business. He had already been to the lodge looking for Tom, and wanted to know where he had been on Saturday night.

Lucy felt completely senseless. She struggled to keep up. It took a few seconds for her to recall that Saturday had been the night of the rugby game and the stolen car. The foreboding that had lodged in her gut for the last day bubbled up again.

Tom was at home that night, she told him cautiously. She had called him there around 10:00 p.m. He asked if Tom had mentioned the car being stolen. She was about to go into details when Ethan put a restraining hand on her back.

"We had the car. It was gone when we came out of the game. We didn't know the registration number and phoned Tom to get it and he said not to bother reporting it right then. He would do it the next morning."

Lucy nodded. "He *must* have reported it."

The detective shook his head, staring at her accusingly.

"He didn't report it. Were you aware the vehicle was unregistered?"

The pressure of Ethan's hand on her back increased. "No. Detective, when we got to the station, there was a queue a mile long and we had restaurant reservations. Tom assured us he would take care of it."

"That car was found at the scene of a suspicious fire."

The rest of the conversation was a blur. The detective asked if anyone could corroborate their story and when Tom would be back. He handed her his card. Lucy closed her eyes in embarrassment when he apologized for interrupting them. When he'd gone, she sagged against the car.

"What's going on, Lucy? Just what's Tom into?"

"I—I don't know," she managed.

"What was that scumbag's name at the rugby?"

"Joseph Dunn. I told Tom. He had to have reported it, for the insurance, right?" With relief, she thought he couldn't file an insurance claim without reporting the car stolen, so no one could accuse him of insurance fraud.

Ethan looked thoughtful. "Maybe this Dunn is trying to set him up."

"But why?"

"Money's my guess. I knew he was in trouble. Didn't realize how deep."

Lucy looked at him sharply. "What do you mean, you knew?"

There was quite a pause. "I've heard some things."

The meat supplier's words that morning flitted around her mind. *Inland Revenue, a private investigator...* "You've heard what? From who?"

"People in the village."

Watch your back... "You've been asking questions about us in the village?"

Ethan rubbed his neck self-consciously. "Magnus asked me to make a few inquiries. He's heard rumors of financial difficulties."

Lucy reeled in the face of his discomfort. He wouldn't—

she'd trusted him. Her lips moved, but she had nothing to say. All she wanted to hear was his denial.

Finally he looked at her and she saw his conscience laid bare. He exhaled. "Magnus takes his club very seriously. He won't tolerate any hint of scandal."

For Lucy, Magnus's expectations were nothing as important as Ethan's role in all this. "Who have you been asking?"

Guilt deepened his tan. "I didn't have to look far."

"Who?" she demanded.

"It's amazing what the locals come up with when you mention where you're staying."

Something in her chest cramped up. There was another long silence while she tried to contain the welling of betrayal. He had spent hours today building her up, showing her he cared and offering his help. Today she had truly felt that anything seemed attainable.

Please, please deny it, she prayed. Deny it, or explain. Give me something…

"It's not to hurt you," he told her softly, reaching out to touch her arm. "That's the last thing—"

She flinched, clamping her arm to her side. "Get out."

Shock and shame and sadness engulfed her. And then the fear. He had the power to destroy them; she had been warned. *Keep your distance, he's all business.*

"Lucy, I want to help."

She shook her head and stepped back. "I want you to go."

"Come upstairs, we'll talk."

Her face flamed with self-disgust when she remembered her impassioned plea of just minutes ago. *Upstairs, now!* "Just go."

Ethan sighed heavily and rubbed his face. After a

long moment when she refused to look at him, he leaned close. "Will you come back to the lodge tonight?"

At the thought of Summerhill, she felt an incredible yearning to be there. To take Monty up to the gorge, to her special place. She wanted peace.

But she carefully erased any sign of interest on her face and instead, faced him with scorn. "Why? Did you think I would sleep with you now?"

It was his turn to flinch. Again he raised his hand toward her. She thrust her chin out defiantly. "Go away." Her voice rang out loud and hard.

Ethan's eyes narrowed but he stepped back. "Cool off for a bit. I'll be back."

Barely able to see where she was going, she walked slowly for the stairs. Her throat closed with anguish. Why would he want to harm her? And why lead her on, fuel her passion, make her feel special and wanted if he were trying to finish off her business?

Because he worked for Magnus. Tom was right. Magnus was intent on getting them off the list. And Ethan was the destroyer.

She leaned on the balustrade, closing her eyes against a painful pounding in her head. This was how her day had started. Confusion and hurt about Ethan and Juliette, fear at the court papers. She had wanted to cry at his thoughtfulness when he'd shown her the brochures from the dyslexia center. Then layer upon layer of approval and admiration, of encouragement and offers of help. An intensity of desire that rocked her—and shocked him also, she was sure.

She shook her bag irritably when she could not locate her key. Muttering mutinously, she tipped the entire contents onto the landing.

In truth, the anger was directed more at herself than

Ethan. It was too late to firewall it. She cared—desperately—about him. She grasped the elusive key in her hand and squeezed it as hard as she could, wincing as it dug into her palm.

And that gave him the power to wound her more deeply than anything had in years. If only she'd kept it professional, but she couldn't even get that right. Why did everything she touched end up in such an unholy mess?

His fingers tapped restlessly on the steering wheel of his rental car. He checked his watch again. Half an hour. She had been in there for half an hour.

His clamorous body had finally subsided after being pushed up to exploding point. The look and feel and smell of her seeped into every corner of his being. Colored everything to the point where he was high when he could see her, and in the depths of depression when he could not.

Only once had he ever felt a fraction of this turmoil for a woman and he'd been barely a man then. She'd been on the swim team at university. But she could not understand his decision to quit swimming when he was a certainty for the Olympics. She could not understand his need to stick to his goals, to exorcise the mess his father had made of everything, and show him that he—Ethan—could do better.

He rubbed his face and checked his watch again. Come on, come on. His hands slapped a drumroll on his thighs. He was so wired. If that detective had not burst in on the scene, he would be deep inside her sweet body now, where he'd wanted to be since the second he first saw her. There would be one more expression to add to his catalog of "Lucy" expressions. He wanted to be an inch away from her face, to watch that sweet mouth curve into a smile of pure satisfaction.

His body signalled its approval of the direction of his thoughts just as his cell phone beeped. It was Clark Seller in the Sydney office.

Clark could barely contain his excitement. The Minister for the Interior for the islands had unexpectedly decided to attend a Pacific Tourism Council in Sydney. He could meet with Ethan tomorrow.

Tomorrow! Damn, damn. Ethan groaned. How could he leave tomorrow without straightening this mess out?

Lucy's face swam in front of his eyes as he'd last seen it. Let down. Scared. He would never have believed himself capable of putting that look on anyone's face. Especially not on her face.

And then his world tipped a little on its axis. It was an indistinct slide of his insides—distant, like a dream in which you're falling over a cliff. A beautiful soundless freefall, without fear—after all, it's just a dream. Right?

Clark's insistent voice intruded and Ethan did something unprecedented. "You handle it."

"What?" Clark was incredulous, but Ethan reassured him that he was more than equipped to handle this preliminary meeting. There would be no negotiations. It was more or less just a feeler.

He hung up and opened the car door. He'd had it with cooling his heels out here.

Lucy's apartment building was beside a busy intersection and the traffic lights had just turned green so he had to wait half a minute to cross the road. The wind was blustery and turned to the south. Bitterly cold, he rubbed his arms as he dodged through the line of stationary vehicles.

He opened the gate and passed through just in time to see the underground garage door closing behind a red sports car. Lucy's red Alfa Romeo.

Cursing, he turned back to fumble at the gate latch just as her car drove right past him.

"Red. Red!" he shouted at the traffic lights and broke into a trot. The lights were not on his side. They went amber and she barrelled through and turned right. Ethan had a near miss with a white utility van as he raced across the road and jumped in his car.

And went nowhere fast. The driver of the van was blocking his way to the far-right lane and the lights stayed red. By the time he finally got going, she must have had nearly five minutes on him. Not being familiar with the one-way-street system in this town cost him precious time and he swore viciously when he ended up going full circle and arrived back outside her apartment building. But at least from here he knew the way to Summerhill.

Where else would she go? Fuming, he raced through the streets and got onto the ring road that led out of the city and toward the West Coast.

Annoyance drilled his temples. Lucy McKinlay had cut him off at the knees. What was he thinking? Turtle Island was his ultimate deal. His biggest, his last, his final revenge. Where was his infamous focus? He was *not* handing over control. No way. This was still his baby.

Come on, Rae. Think! He held engineering and business degrees. Solving problems was his forte. Political, legal, employment—how could one small personal dilemma slip under his grid and turn his lights out?

It was an utterly wretched ninety-minute drive with no sign of her car ahead, but there was more than one route to the mountains. Finally the turn-off to the ski village flashed by and he decelerated. The weather was closing in fast. Ethan thought fleetingly of the hunting party and hoped they were home safe.

Soon, on the long driveway up to the lodge, he caught sight of a flash of red by the stables and swung the steering wheel that way. Surely she would not be fool enough to go riding when dusk was on them and a storm was brewing.

It must have been zero degrees with a windchill factor of formidable proportions when he alighted. The rain was just starting in earnest—big, fat skin-shrinking drops with the promise of more. He ducked his head and raced for the stable entrance.

Lucy sat huddled with her knees drawn up to her chin in a corner of Monty's stall. Her face was a mixture of sullen surprise and resignation.

"No." Ethan shook his head.

Petulantly she jerked to her feet. "I know that. Leave me alone." She froze him with a look of such disdain, he hardly registered that she'd pushed past him.

Her turning her back on him, walking away, sharpened his temper. Frustration gnawed at him, born of the simmering sexual tension he had kept reined in all this long day. He made a grab for her arm, but she easily shook him off and walked out into the night. It took him a few seconds to register she had just walked out on him—again—and then he followed, almost disbelieving.

Icy rain slashed at his face the moment he was out the door. The wind howled, buffeting him. Such was the deluge, it took him a while to make her out because he, naturally, was looking toward their vehicles.

Lucy, unpredictably, had stomped off in the direction of the house with her arms wrapped around herself.

She still wore a light knit top and a leather jacket that was more stylish than protective against the elements.

His temper surged, warming him. He ducked his head and set off after her, snagging her arm in a vice-like grip. It was hard to make out her face in the gathering darkness and driving rain, but her eyes flashed dangerously.

"Leave me alone!"

He pulled her to a standstill. "Get in the car."

She attempted to release her arm, to no avail. "Just what is your agenda, Ethan?" Her voice surged and faded as the wind whipped parts of the question away.

"Right now, it's to get out of this blasted storm. Get in the car."

She pulled away, successfully this time, swearing colorfully.

"Spoiled brat!" he yelled after her in complete exasperation.

With a resigned glance at the two cars parked outside the stables, he caught up to her and fell into step beside her. It was slow going into the teeth of the driving southerly and both of them hunched over grimly, not looking at each other.

"Stop running away from me," he demanded through clenched teeth.

"You stop running after me," she retorted. "Why are you trying to hurt Summerhill?" She pulled up smartly and faced him.

"I'm not." He took his hand from his pocket and turned her toward the house, urging her on. "It's my job, Lucy. Do you really think Magnus doesn't suspect what's going on here? That's why he asked me to look into it."

"So you admit it." She shook her dripping head in

disgust. "You're running around digging up dirt so you can kick us out of the club."

"It's not like that. I can help you."

"We don't need *your* help," she snapped, but her voice sounded decidedly shaky now.

Ethan swiped at the water streaming down his face, and peered at her. Her pale hair was plastered to her head. In the glow of the house lights, ten meters away, her eyes were dark smudges, the color of the storm.

His heart lurched and squeezed. Ah, Lucy, what are you doing to me? He planted his feet stubbornly.

"You being nice to me today." Her voice shook. "Giving me the rope to hang myself. Making me trust you so I'll tell you what Magnus needs to get us off the list."

He rocked back on his heels. "Wrong."

"You're using me to cover up your affair with Juliette."

The sour taste of injustice flooded his throat. "Wrong again. But there are problems here."

"If you take us off the Global List, we're finished."

"The situation isn't irretrievable. I can make Magnus see that."

She turned away from him again. "Maybe you won't be Magnus's golden-haired boy when he knows that you're his wife's lover."

Her foot was on the bottom step of the veranda before he hauled on her arm. "For the last time, I am *not* Juliette's lover."

"Oh, bugger off!" She poured all her strength into freeing her arm, but he held fast and turned her.

"Listen to me. Someone sent me some newspaper clippings a few days ago. Juliette was investigated for the death of her first husband. No charges in the end, but I had to make sure."

Lucy's mouth dropped open.

Ethan took advantage of her momentary immobilization to move a step closer. "I had to check it out but I couldn't get her on her own here. So I followed you down south."

She swallowed, her eyes as big as saucers. "You thought she…?"

He nodded. "She threw me out. But I talked to her here last night. She went through hell as tabloid fodder for two years. Even though there was no evidence, everyone in the States thought she was guilty. That's why she moved to Australia. New name, new age, new husband."

"Why didn't you tell me? Does Magnus know?"

Ethan put his hands on her shoulders. "That's why I didn't tell you. He's bound to find out at some stage. She made me swear not to say anything until she's had a chance to talk to him."

"Do you believe her?"

He nodded. "Yeah, I do. She's a nice lady who's had a rough time. Do you believe me?"

Lucy wrapped her arms about herself. "So you're not having an affair with your boss's wife?"

He shook his head.

She held his gaze, her chin raised. There was a mighty struggle in her face. The desire to believe him warring with distrust. The hunger for his words to be true. Had she never trusted, never felt supported?

He grabbed her hands in his. "Let's get it all out in the open. All of it." He turned her and pushed her up the remaining steps, out of the deluge. At the door, he put his hands in her hair, combing it back with his fingers, squeezing the moisture out. "Lucy, I *don't* want Juliette, but I *do* want you. I *have* been asking questions, but I'll do everything I can to help." He touched her face gently. "I'm worried, Lucy. I'm worried that your brother is in over his head and dragging you down with him."

She nodded. "I'm a little scared, too. I had a visitor this morning, the lodge's former meat supplier, before you arrived. He's already got a judgment from the civil court for unpaid accounts. Now he's threatening to put us into liquidation."

Ethan swore under his breath. He knew from his inquiries that the rot had spread a lot farther than the local butcher. "No wonder you were upset this morning."

She looked up at him, dripping and shaking with cold. "Tom just runs rings around me lately. He won't tell me what's wrong."

He pulled her close. "We'll sort it out." He felt her head bump against his chest and heard her muffled "Okay."

Fierce with relief, he crushed her to him. She shivered, and it went bone-deep as his arms pressed her saturated clothes to her body. Then he lifted her off the ground and against him. "You're driving me mad," he muttered. "It's all wrong, but God help me, Lucy, I want you. Only you."

And then he was kissing her deeply with a hunger that was more to do with feeding a soul than assuaging a need.

They made puddles on the step. "We need to get you warm," he told her when he noticed she was practically shivering out of the circle of his arms. "Inside."

He followed her up the stairs, holding her hand, knowing he was walking headlong into repercussions. They passed his room, her boots squelching in time with his thumping heart. Once he entered her room, there would be no going back.

She stopped at a door on the other side of the second floor from the guest accommodation. Lucy could hardly open the door, she was shaking so much.

"Shower." She pointed to the bathroom as he closed her door.

Ethan put his hands on her hips and walked her ahead of him into the bathroom. The decision was made. He wouldn't shy from it—he would face it with his usual consummate efficiency. There had to be a way to fit this vital and growing need for her in with achieving his goals.

Reaching into the stall, he turned the shower on. Lucy flipped the fan heater on and shed her soaked-through jacket and boots while he lifted two big towels from the top of the vanity and threw them on the floor. And when steam began fogging up the glass shower door, he pushed her gently inside the stall, kicked off his shoes and followed himself.

Lucy's eyes closed in bliss as the strong jet of hot water rained over her, seeping through her clothes. A sigh, deep and tremulous, rose from her lips and eased his tension somewhat. She let the spray run on her back for a minute then pulled him close so he could enjoy it, too. Together they faced the spray. His hands began rubbing, in short, hard strokes down her back and sides.

Minutes passed and finally her shaking subsided. She looked around in wonder, as if she wasn't sure how she came to be in this place. In her shower, fully clothed and with him. And then her eyes warmed as she focused on him.

Ethan's blood began to hum. Fear, distrust, betrayal, all extinguished now. He'd seen this in her eyes today also, on the wall by the sea and later in the car. Heavy-lidded, pupils dilated with sultry awareness. His body took that last leap into an adrenaline-drenched response.

His hands felt as useless as frozen legs of lamb as he peeled her top over her head. Rose-pink lace with pale green ribbon; the sight of her bra erased any thought of Turtle Island or repercussions. Suddenly the only relevant detail he craved was whether her underwear matched.

For about one second, until Lucy reached behind her and flicked her bra free with one hand. Now he was just impatient to see the rest of her. He helped push the bra up and off her shoulders.

He wanted his hands on her, but his focus did seem to be skew-whiff at the present. He was momentarily halted by her fingers at his shirt, and he would have to say she won in the dexterity stakes. All buttons undone in the time it took for him to undo the snap at the waist-band of her jeans.

Ethan slid the heavy denim down her legs and took her panties with them. Did they match? He couldn't remember because by then, he was running his hands up the back of her legs, amazed at how long and lithe they were for someone so small. He really must slow and pay attention, but he did not want to miss a single second, or bypass a single inch of her. He wanted to see and taste and feel everything.

As he stood to full height, his hands stopped on her behind. Smooth, curved, a delicious handful. Lucy meanwhile, busied herself with his slacks and Ethan let out a careful breath as he was freed completely from the shackles of wet clothing.

Finally naked—and for a little while, it seemed enough just to look. With his hands cupping her bottom and hers resting on his chest, his mind was at peace with the confessions and decisions of the last hour.

Her skin had the soft luster of pearl. Her arms and shoulders were delicate, her body slim but not angular. Sweetly rounded curves next to his long slashing lines of lean muscle. So many contrasts, not only to him but to anyone he'd been with before. Mostly, he felt so big next to her small frame.

Water cascaded down her face and body and she shimmered like the fairy he had thought of when he first saw her. Her small hands rested flat on his chest, providing yet another shocking contrast to his own coloring.

Need for her rolled through him, burst out in a ragged exhalation. He placed his hands on hers—they were warm now—and felt his own heart pumping through them. Ethan shut the water off and backed out of the shower, pulling her with him. He swathed them both in one large soft towel.

They maneuvered into the bedroom still bound in the towel. Lucy's cheeks were rosy, her breathing quick. He pulled the towel closer around them, warm, damp bodies bumping against each other as they jostled.

Light drifted in from the living room and combined with the open bathroom door to cast an eerie glow. Ethan looked around the big room, his gaze halting at an armchair by the window with a stuffed toy holding a balloon. His heart stopped. Raising his hands to his head he pulled the towel down over his face, swearing succinctly.

"What is it?"

He looked down into her face, shook his head wryly. "We have to go to my room."

"Your room?"

"Condoms." His face screwed up into a grimace. "I had a couple in my wallet, which is still in the car. But I have some in my case."

Lucy smiled easily and opened her mouth to speak. Then a muted flash of orange lit the room, snagging her attention. Next thing he knew, she had twisted away, leaving him clutching an armful of damp towel and nothing else.

She ran over to the window, dragging aside heavy drapes. "Look!"

Nine

Lucy waited for another stab of lightning. There was a young magnolia to the left of her window, its branches reaching just below her sill. Right now, it whipped about gracefully. The storm had worsened while they were in the shower.

The music of it enthralled her. The wind howled menacingly and she felt the eaves of the old house vibrate under the force of it. The rain was heavy and hard on the old iron roof. And something deeper—a long roll of thunder, not too far away. She closed down a quick, skimming thought that it rumbled a warning.

The tree thrashed in a flamboyant dance. Its branches reached up in an entreaty. Will I? Do I trust him enough? She sensed Ethan come up behind her and she began to sway with the wind. Then a great flash of sheet lightning lit the room up again. Lucy laughed in pure delight.

He moved in close and put his hands around her

waist. They looked almost black against her paleness. She put her hands on top of his and leaned back into his warmth, still swaying. The thunder rolled on, making the house shudder—or maybe it was just her. The lightning continued to strike, moving around the valley in an arc.

Their reflection in the window danced, faded, surged, like her thoughts, her fears, the need piercing her. Thousands of raindrops raced each other down the glass. He was hard to see in the window because he was so dark. As she swayed, they moved in time to the rhythm she created. Their hands were light on her body and her movement meant they slid over her, branding her with the touch she directed.

The storm noise intensified to a crescendo any orchestra would have been proud of. It seemed the lightning, having belted every valley and hill and mountain and gorge around Summerhill, was now coming for the house itself. Confrontation. She glimpsed the stables and outbuildings as they lit up, a beacon of courage. But then their reflections shifted.

Nestling her head into his throat, her arms slid behind her to pull him closer. His hands firmed on their teasing exploration of her abdomen and rib cage. At the very moment his fingers brushed over the tingling tips of her breasts, she felt the unmistakable thickness of him push between her thighs. Trance-like, she watched their reflections melting into the rain trailing down the windowpane. Lightning seemed to strike and flow from his eyes.

"Are you the devil?" she breathed.

His teeth flashed in a brief smile, then he was kissing her neck while his fingers pinched and stroked her nipples. Lucy's insides melted and started to flow and

she squeezed her thighs, trapping him. His groan puffed
hot into her ear.

Then the shock of him gliding hot and hard against
her blurred the blasts of lightning. A ragged sob washed
from her throat as the heavens poured down outside. A
distant rolling tension started deep down, relentless as
the thunder. Gone were all thoughts of consequences or
the future—she surrendered to the storm within.

Ethan nipped into her neck and she rocked back
against him, her breasts filling his palms. Man, this was
heaven, and he never wanted to stop.

She swayed and undulated against his shaft and then
loosened her grip. Hot as lava. He groaned. This was
hell, and he needed more.

Keeping one hand on her breast, he moved the other
down to stroke the smooth skin of her bottom, gently
tugging then pushing back to create a delicious rhyth-
mic friction for both of them. Her ragged gasp, his
heavy one, added to the turbulence outside.

Another clout of lightning lit the room and she
leaned forward, with only his hand at her breast to stop
her toppling. And he knew what she wanted. Him. Inside her now, like this. From behind.

He wanted that, too. But her face…it was a promise
he'd made to himself. To watch her come apart.

And storm or no storm, he did not do unprotected
sex; it wasn't part of the plan.

Sensing his impending withdrawal, she clamped her
legs together, whimpering a denial. He persisted—
sweet agony—and turned her. She gulped air. There
was nothing sleepy about her eyes now. Demanding,
fierce with need. Their bodies surged together, mouths
seeking, sucking, sampling. Her arms were around his

neck. Rock-hard nipples chafed his rib cage, which dragged another groan of impatience from his throat. If she didn't stop, he'd lose it.

She didn't stop. She pushed against him and, unprepared, he stepped back. And again. She had a plan but his mouth was too busy, too full of her to ask. She kept pushing till they reached her bedside table and she yanked open the drawer and pressed something into his hand. Then she hauled herself up against him, pressing and swaying and rubbing.

He fumbled with the packet, the blood roaring in his ears. She moved one hand down between them to help. He pressed her hand into his side with his arm. Not helping!

In the few seconds it took to sheath himself, he dragged in a lungful of air and tried to slow things. Ethan was at ease with the act of love, if not the emotion. If ever he could be generous, make it special, it should be now. Because he cared now as he'd never done before.

He forced himself to block out the lithe body gyrating against him, those impatient little breaths deep in her throat and her busy hands roaming and stroking. His arms slid around her waist and he drew her close, smiling tightly at the impatience in her eyes.

"Easy," he murmured.

Then his mouth took hers so deeply, so possessively, he swallowed her protest and she sagged against him.

She hadn't reckoned on being gentled, he guessed. He molded her body against him, inhaled the clean warmth of her, swayed with her and felt the hum deep in her throat. As his tongue teased over and under hers, she stilled and accepted.

But only for a few seconds. What she then did to his tongue should have been a felony. In a shock of disintegrating control, he imagined that part of her, the mouth that he dreamed about, on another part of his body, mimicking that motion. That other part of his body that was now straining between them, demanding critical attention.

His hands moved down to the back of her thighs and he braced and lifted her against him. Her legs instantly locked around his waist.

And then she did it. Reached down and cupped him while sliding up and down against him. Before his knees buckled, he turned and they fell on the bed with a *whump!*

He buried his mouth into the fragrant hollow at the base of her throat, inhaling deeply. When her arms tightened around his back, he raised his head. The eerie flashing of the lightning clouded her eyes. He touched his lips to hers, a soft whisper of a kiss, at the instant he slid into her body. Both of them exhaled, stilled.

So hot. The pleasure of being deep inside her was all concentrated there in a burst of tingling vibrations. For moments he lay, holding his breath, letting his body breathe for him. He felt a single thread of steel form and run the length of his insides, pulling tighter and tighter.

Their eyes were locked on each other's, building an immeasurable, searing passion. His surprise at the intensity of it glowed in her eyes. It robbed them of breath, girding them for something a little dangerous, but vital and inevitable.

Then Lucy hissed in a quick breath through her nose and licked the corner of his mouth. "Not easy," she pleaded.

Lifting slightly, he took some weight on his knees and slipped his hands under her buttocks. Then she lifted her hips jerkily and his descent into the storm began.

She met him eagerly, triumph glowing in her eyes. He pulled her body up against him with every stroke. Within the confines of her body, there were no limits, only rising layers of euphoria. In one deep stroke, he could feel her boundaries. With the next, he floundered as she stretched and flowed and tightened around him. He forgot everything else. This was all that mattered. Lucy, here, under him.

Their hips whipped like well-oiled pistons, smooth, deep, in complete tandem. A dizzying surge of vibrations plucked at the steel thread inside, quivering to every extremity. In a mind that was rapidly being obliterated by raw sensation, Ethan sensed a sultry, subtle change. From warm inside to drenchingly blazing hot.

She was close. She surged against him and he arched his back as her nails dug deeply into his flesh, urging him on. She was close and he needed to see, but her head had rolled to the side. He would not let her hide. He breathed her name, once, then again, louder. She turned her face and her eyes snapped open.

Lightning slashed through the window again and Ethan got what he wanted. Lucy, helplessly crying out against his mouth, unable to contain the flow of ecstasy.

Ethan pitched headlong into the storm and soared out over the valley. He felt the thread snap and blow the back of his head out, then streak through him to blast out of the soles of his feet.

She ripped his guts, his heart out.

They stretched on their sides in her bed, sighing in pleasure, freed from the shackles of a shrieking tension built up over days—decades—of need.

Several long minutes passed and their breathing returned to normal. Moving her head to the side, she peered at him drowsily. "You are the devil," she whispered, licking her parched lips.

His eyes fixed on her face, brightening with humor. "You're not quite the angel I thought you were."

"What makes you say that?"

"Could have something to do with a big box of…" He turned his head to squint at a box lying on its side in the open drawer of her bedside table. His arm rose and he twisted it around. "*Sixty* condoms…"

"It was a joke," she protested mildly. "A farewell present from a silly friend in New York."

His head sank back onto the pillow and the bed shook with his lazy laughter.

Lucy giggled. "It was fun coming through customs. I haven't used any of them, till now."

He crooked an eyebrow.

"Six months."

"Honored." His head inclined in a salute.

He turned her palm. "Who was your last?" Then he pressed his lips to it. "Was he special?"

That one little act brought a rush of emotion to her throat. Way to make a girl feel special, she thought.

They sat up, arranged pillows behind their heads and pulled the duvet over them.

"He was my tutor. I'd started a film-making course in New York, paid for, as usual by my poor father."

She stretched and put her arms behind her head.

Lucy had had one or two promising relationships before Jerry, but she'd learned at an early age that to expect love just because you gave it was setting yourself up for a fall. Sure enough, one day she discovered she was far from the first of his students to have gone down that road.

From there, she ceased to see herself as a love interest, realizing she was one in a long line of gullible girls. The thrill was gone. She ended the relationship and abandoned the course.

"What made you come home?" Ethan asked, stroking her hair.

"The break-up with Jerry sort of coincided with Dad's stroke." She turned into him and snuggled under his chin. "I suddenly realized how aimless and self-serving my life was. And failing on the course. That was the third course Dad had shelled out for over the years."

"Poor little rich girl." He dropped a kiss on her head.

"I never did get the chance to tell him I was sorry. I mean, I did, but after the stroke. Who knows whether he understood."

Those first few days after the stroke still haunted her. Her father was so confused about what was happening to him. He would stare at his useless hand, his uncooperative leg. He had stared at her, too, as if he could not place her.

"Maybe *he* should have told *you* he was sorry."

It was his tone that lifted her head. "What did he have to be sorry about?"

"For neglecting you all those years, blaming you for what your mother did to him." His voice was quiet. "Sounds to me like he didn't deserve your compassion."

She laid her head down again and snuggled in closer. They listened to the rain beat loudly on the roof and the wind keen. Lucy felt she never wanted to move from here.

"You do realize—" Ethan put his hand under her chin and tilted her face up to him "—being naughty, charming your way through life—it's all just a cry for attention."

She blinked at him. How did he see that so quickly? It had taken her some years to figure that out.

A tiny spurt of something broke inside her. It was so unexpected, so unfamiliar, it almost hurt. She'd have called it hope if she hadn't crushed it down ruthlessly, as was her habit.

She'd long since given up hope of a kind word from her father, a kiss or cuddle like she'd had when she was small, before Belle had left. Long since given up hope of a fairy-tale love. It was best that way. She was living proof. The *love* word made people run—her faster than most.

She leaned close and kissed his chest. She would enjoy tonight. Tomorrow would come. For now, keep things nice and easy.

He lifted her chin toward him again. "Let's make a plan."

She grinned, shaking her head. "You and your plans."

His index finger traced the shape of her lips. "You are very beautiful," he murmured. "And you were not part of the plan."

No, Lucy thought sadly. I never am. But her smile didn't slip.

"Told you about Turtle Island, didn't I? It's going to be huge. It's going to be the premier luxury resort in the world. It's also going to take up most of my time over the next couple of years."

Her heart sank even as hope burgeoned inside. And again, she quelled it. Don't get your hopes up. He's already talking about leaving, and that will be that.

"But the islands are only three or four hours away. You can come visit. We'll drink kava in the sun."

"That's a nice idea," Lucy told him brightly and, as was her way, pushed the maudlin thoughts aside.

"Get an assessment done, Lucy. Soon. I'll get those

business plans drawn up, we will sort out this mess with Tom, and you can start putting some of those ideas into effect. You do own fifty per cent of this operation."

She sighed. "He won't listen."

"He damned well will. There's more to you than he thinks. Let's show him."

Let's. What a small, inconsequential word. She tried to picture it in her mind, the shape of it, the number of letters. From his mouth, it meant *two.* Two of them. Together. Us.

Hope and longing flared again. Get it out of your mind. She rubbed her cheek up under his chin. He could use a shave. She could use some sense.

She looked down his relaxed body. So long, so strong. Her hand smoothed the light sprinkling of hair on his broad chest. What a view.

A muscle in his upper thigh twitched. Lucy turned her head to lick at his nipple, see it respond. Her finger glided slowly lower, over his tawny belly. She raised her face again, and nibbled on the bristles along his jawline. They kissed, deep and lingering. His arms tightened and she felt his hands spread wide. Her heart stuttered.

Much later, the sounds of his ecstasy trickled from his lips after a torturously slow and gentle seduction. He smoothed her hair, still looking intently into her eyes. Something flowed between them—a sensation as lush and complex as a fine wine. He'd filled her with a million pinpricks of light and sweetness that swelled and burst and streamed through her with agonizing slowness.

It was the best—and the worst—she had ever felt. She tore her gaze away and pushed him and curled up hard into him. Whimpering with gratification, she hoped he did not notice the couple of baffling tears she shed.

* * *

They dressed haphazardly and wandered downstairs in search of food, barefoot and holding hands. The electrical storm had long passed but heavy rain and high winds still lashed the house. Lucy's quiet and sultry chatter checked at the sound of distress in the kitchen. They opened the door to find Ellie, Summerhill's housekeeper, calling into the radiotelephone, looking and sounding agitated.

Lucy moved to her side immediately. "What is it?"

Ellie stared at her. "What are you doing here?" She broke off to look at Ethan, a puzzled line appearing between her brows as she took in their disheveled appearance. "I thought you were in town. Your car…"

"It's down at the stables. Ellie, what's wrong?"

"Oh, Lucy, it's a terrible mess. There's been an accident."

Ellie spoke into the RT in her hand. "Summerhill to Tom, can you hear me, Tom?"

Another faint crackle, nothing intelligible. The older woman looked at Lucy's worried face. "I got the first call about ten. His radio was wet and running out of power. There was a landslide. The hut they were in— Craiglea—was nearly wiped out. They decided to try to make it to the ford. Tom said it wasn't too bad at that stage. But he was wrong. From what I can make out, one or both Jeeps were washed into the river in a flash flood."

"Oh no," Lucy whispered.

"Anyone hurt?" Ethan demanded.

"The signal was weak, but I don't think so. I think he said they all ended up in the water and have lost everything, rifles, food, wet-weather gear, the lot. He saved just the one radio."

Lucy and Ethan stared at each other. Guilt radiated between them. While they'd been enjoying themselves, they hadn't given a thought to the hunting party. And now those people, people close to them, were in danger.

"Search and Rescue, Ellie, have you called them?"

Ellie nodded. "The local police are tied up. There's flooding right along the river. They have sent for police from town to assess the situation."

"Are there other huts?" Ethan asked tersely.

"Which side of the river, Ellie?"

"Mountain side. Fernlea would be the closest."

Lucy looked at Ellie in consternation. "That's miles. They'll never make it in this weather on foot."

Even as she said that, something niggled in her brain, some long-distant memory. She pushed it aside to listen to Ellie.

"Not easy to find either. It's straight up into the hills. Stupid, stupid." She tsked. "Why didn't they stay put at Craiglea? Made the best of it? I talked to Tom at three, soon as I knew the storm was on the way. He wanted to show Mr. Anderson one more spot."

"Any ideas, Ellie?"

The older woman inhaled, looking at each of them in turn. "We stay put and wait. It's up to the police to decide if Search and Rescue can attempt a river crossing in the dark while the storm is still going on. We'll just have to hope Tom and the others can find some shelter and keep warm."

"How many of them?" Ethan asked, looking at Lucy.

"Tom, Stacey, Magnus and Mr. Endo, one of the other guests."

"Oh, my," Ellie suddenly exclaimed. "I suppose we should tell Mrs. Anderson and Mrs. Endo. I've talked to Marie, Stacey's wife."

"I'll go to Juliette, you take Mrs. Endo. Ethan, put some coffee on. And keep an ear out for the radio."

"Shouldn't we go after them?" Ethan asked.

Ellie shook her head adamantly. "There's enough fool folk in the bush for one night. The police should be here soon. Just pray this storm lets up."

Ten

Ethan made a big pot of coffee and fiddled with the radio, to no avail. Soon Juliette and the Indonesian woman joined him and Lucy and Ellie in the kitchen. Juliette confessed to lying awake worrying about the storm. Ethan felt sorry for the Indonesian woman. Her English was poor and there was no way of knowing how much she understood.

While they waited for the police he and Lucy braved the rain to check on the horses. To their horror, the river, two hundred meters away, was now within a meter of the stables. It took them nearly an hour to lead the half dozen animals back up to the barn where the Jeeps were kept, and to move their cars out of reach of the water.

A two-man team of police experienced in mountain search and rescue arrived, reporting widespread flooding for miles around. The weather was still atrocious. They spread maps all over the big kitchen table. Lucy stepped back, admitting that maps were beyond her, and Ellie showed them Tom's last known location. The area was steep and densely forested. After an hour's deliberation and calls to local search and rescue personnel, it was decided to wait until daybreak to attempt to send a team across the river.

Hour after hour they waited. At about four in the morning, Ethan left the cops in the kitchen and stretched out on one of the couches in the lounge. He scraped his hand along his jaw and thought he must look like hell.

Lucy sat across from him, talking to Juliette. Lucy looked utterly adorable. Her hair had been saturated and dried so many times today—not to mention enduring a sexathon—that it spiked out in all directions. She looked like a trendy hairdresser with a sticky-product fetish. Except that she wore a blue check shirt and jeans and woolly socks—the perfect farm girl.

The women talked quietly and his eyelids drifted shut. Nothing to be done till the morning. He might as well sleep.

He heard Juliette tell Lucy she couldn't bear having to bury another husband. She talked of her first husband and the night that had changed her life, pitching her into a living hell for two years. Lucy did not let on that she already knew about it.

"I've paid my dues. I just want to be with Magnus for as long as we have and be pampered and pamper him back. Is that so wrong?"

"No, of course not. Doesn't he know…?"

"I'll tell him, as soon as he…" Juliette's voice hitched. "I was foolish to think I could hide it.

"I know people think I'm a gold digger." The sadness in her voice was evident.

Ethan would not have done anything differently. The

newspaper clippings needed to be checked out. But he was glad things had turned out both for Juliette and his friend.

She continued sadly. "Truth is, I love him to bits and I'm proud to be his wife. I would never cheat on him. Growing up dirt-poor, I know I have a lot to be grateful for, and I am."

"It's obvious how close you are," Lucy murmured.

"It's not a one-way street. He gets his masculinity fed. He's proud to have me on his arm. And he was so lonely when I met him. Now he laughs all the time. I make him laugh."

Ethan had to agree with that.

"He also loves giving things. He's generous. And he has someone to fuss over him now, make sure he takes his pills.

"But all some people see is he'll be dead in a few short years, and I will still be young, and rich."

"Not the ones that know you both, surely," Lucy protested.

Ethan heard a mirthless chuckle. "People get jealous, I'm living a dream life."

There was a pause, and drowsiness pressed down on his mind.

"You must see a lot of rich old men through here, honey. Tell me you never thought about it—snagging one and being obscenely rich."

Ethan inhaled sharply through his nostrils, held it. Time stood still for a moment, or seemed to in his mind. He opened his eyes, somewhat reluctantly.

Lucy was grinning. "Oh, yeah. All the time."

She's joking, he told himself.

"Sadly, most of them bring their wives."

She must be…

"Their trophy wives," Juliette sighed.

"Ethan said that," Lucy said cheerily. She turned her head and looked at him. On seeing his eyes open, she smiled an intimate little smile. "Oh. You're awake."

Ethan relaxed. She had a hell of a smile. He drank it in and smiled back.

Juliette stood and stretched. "I need some aspirin."

Lucy rose also. "I'll get you some."

Juliette said she had plenty in her room and excused herself. Lucy came over to Ethan's couch and perched on the edge. She expressed grave fears for the farm animals on the grazing land close to the river. They agreed that as soon as the search and rescue team was dispatched, they would go check on the stock. From what they had seen by the stables, the river had burst its banks in a big way. There could be substantial losses.

At five-thirty, the rest of the search and rescue team arrived. It was dark and still raining heavily, but the wind had dropped.

The team discussed their options over coffee and Ellie's warm date scones. Lucy stood behind the seated men, chewing on her bottom lip worriedly, but she suddenly snapped her fingers. "Ellie, did you say Tom tried to cross at the ford?"

She had remembered something: an old Department of Conservation hut. "Tom would know of it. It's not used anymore. They might have headed there for shelter."

"Are you sure it's in this area?" the team leader asked.

"I stayed there once, camping out, when I was a kid. All I know is, it's only about half an hour's ride on the other side of the ford, in a big stand of pine."

"May not even be still standing," Ellie said dubiously.

"It's worth a shot," one of the men said. "How deep is the ford usually?"

"Usually only one, one and a half feet, but…" Lucy shrugged again.

Ethan guessed the whole landscape would have changed in this storm. The radio news said it was the worst flood in the area for fifty years.

A rescue helicopter from town was already on alert. As soon as it was light, it would be flown to the top of the gorge. One team would climb from there down into the stand of pine it was hoped the hunters were holed up in. Another team would drive to the ford—if that were possible—and attempt a river crossing, then up through the bush to the vicinity of the hut.

The condition of the hunters and the safety of the river crossing or the climb would determine how the party would be brought out.

As soon as it was light, the team set off, promising to keep in touch by radiotelephone. Ethan and Lucy stood on the veranda and stared in shock at the unfamiliar look of the terrain in front of the house. The normally benign Rakaia had spread into a huge lake that encroached up past the stables. It wasn't so deep, but the area it covered was impressive.

"Lucky you thought to move the horses," Ethan murmured.

"We'd better feed them. Then I'll call the neighbor. Apparently he looks after a lot of our stock, and I hope he'll know where they are."

According to the news, many of the lower-lying farms in the district had been flooded, and not just pasture. Summerhill was lucky because the house was on a rise. There were several properties with a couple of feet of water flowing through. They also still had phone access and power, unlike some of the more remote properties.

Lucy called their nearest neighbor and discovered he had been up for hours and had already seen to most of the animals on his and Summerhill's land. "There's just one group of ours he's a bit worried about—down in the south pasture. He thinks there's around fifty head there. But the land does rise at one end. He hopes the animals have made their way to the top.

"He offered to go check," she continued. "But I'm tired of sitting around the house worrying. I'll go."

Ellie fixed them a big breakfast and shortly after eight, Lucy saddled up Monty and the mare Tilley for Ethan. They were well wrapped up in oilskins, boots and gloves and Lucy made Ellie promise to call her on her cell phone the moment any news came in from the rescue team.

"Lead on, cowgirl." Ethan grinned, saluting her.

They set off into the dim morning, heavy rain making conversation difficult. Lucy was in awe at the massive lake the river had made of her land. It was sluggish and not deep but they had to take care in the dips and valleys. Luckily she had a good memory and guided them confidently to the pasture they were seeking, about an hour's ride from the house.

Three hours later, they had nearly all of the cattle herded into the gardens around the lodge, to Ellie's dismay. They saw only two dead cattle in the floodwaters, and one trembling beast had to be roped and hauled up out of a water-filled hole. Then they rode over to check on the neighbor.

Ellie rang while they were still there to say the hunting party were all alive and well and had made it safely across the river. Tom was the only one with an injury—a suspected broken wrist. They had indeed sheltered in the old DOC hut. Lucy's recollection had saved hours of searching.

"Hell of a memory you got there." Ethan gave her a high five and she pushed her hood back and grinned with relief.

They set off for home midafternoon. Weary as he was, his muscles protesting at the unaccustomed hours in the saddle, Ethan looked around in wonder at the damage Mother Nature could inflict. He had previously experienced the other end of the spectrum, where she refused to provide *any* water, the greatest necessity of life.

Lucy seemed to be ambling along at half his pace. He reined in and waited, struck by her desolate expression. She was looking around, not at the flooding but the gorge and the mountains. She looked at it as if she'd never see it again.

"Great country, Lucy."

"Even like this," she agreed. "You know, I loved traveling, but wherever in the world I was, however hard I looked, Summerhill has always been the most exotic place for me." She looked at him curiously. "Do you have an exotic place? Somewhere you keep locked away inside?"

Wherever you are, he thought promptly, and clamped his mouth shut before he made a complete ass of himself. He shook his head.

They moved off.

"I guess I'm dreading seeing Magnus."

Ethan tried to suppress a smile. "His bark's worse than his bite."

They continued on in silence for a minute, the horses stirring up squelching mud in the waterlogged pasture.

"If he takes us off the Global List, Tom wants to sell," she told him suddenly.

He pulled to a stop. "Sell the lodge?" he asked in surprise.

She shook her head. "The land, not the lodge. He's never cared about the land." The desolate expression was back.

"How do you feel about that?"

Lucy gave a barely-there rise of her shoulders. "I've always found the house a bit depressing since Mum left. Every minute I could, I'd be out here, riding, camping, just walking. I couldn't bear it if he sold even an inch of it."

Ethan scratched his head. What a load on her shoulders at the moment. "You must have a say."

"I can't tell him what to do with his fifty per cent."

He nodded and thought for a few moments. He had nothing to do with Magnus's club or the Global List, but he knew that Magnus took it very seriously indeed. "I'll talk to him, but I can't promise anything. Magnus would probably overlook some things. It's the hint of financial embarrassment that could be the sticking point. I know he's heard rumors. The sort of people that belong to the club don't like rumors."

Lucy nodded, sighing heavily. Ethan stared at her mouth, wanting to kiss her troubles away. "Lucy, if you're out of the club, it's not the end of the world. With the right marketing, you can still run a good business."

"The prestige of it is a big thing with Tom. But the main reason is the exclusive advertising rights. We won't have time to build a new market and be able to trade our way out of debt before—before it's too late."

He didn't want to tell her that as far as creditors went, the meat supplier she already knew about was in the basket named peanuts. There was a whole lot worse to come.

"Cheer up. We'll talk to him tonight and then I can work on Magnus. But if I can't swing it, I'll set up something with my marketing team. We can't get you into all the printed accommodation publications over-night, but there are lots of ways to target your market that get results in months rather than years."

"Really?" She looked up at him hopefully and his heart squeezed. Tom and her father had kept her down for so long. No wonder her confidence was shot. She needed to know that anything was possible.

She needed to know he would help.

She was already perking up. "Hey, you're not too bad on that horse, for a city slicker," she told him with a big grin.

"Kid, I was riding when you were still a twinkle in your daddy's eye."

"You reckon?" She laughed and leaned over to give him a playful push. And somehow lost her balance, ending up flat on her back in a pool of mud.

Ethan grabbed Monty's bridle to bring him to a standstill so he didn't step on Lucy. "Jesus! You okay?"

She lay there for a couple of seconds, a surprised look on her face. When she started to gurgle with laugh-ter, he relaxed.

"I dare you to laugh." She gasped.

His mouth tightened with the effort of not smiling. He couldn't do anything about the sparkle in his eyes. "Wouldn't dream of it," he told her solemnly.

Leaning down, he put out his hand. She grabbed it, but before she hauled herself up out of the mud, she squinted up at him. "You know," she said, matter-of-factly, "just for a moment, you sitting up there tall enough to touch the sky, you reminded me of my father when I was little."

He gestured at his hand, indicating she get up. "There's a worrying thought."

Lucy giggled as she was hauled up to her feet and

stood, swaying slightly with one hand on Monty's back. She took off one glove and wiped her hair, grimacing at the sludge that appeared on her hand.

"Even with you looking like something the cat dragged in," Ethan continued as she heaved herself up into the saddle, "I am definitely not harboring any fatherly feelings toward you."

They arrived back at Summerhill to find the hunters were home, except for Tom who was at the local medical center having his wrist X-rayed. Magnus and Juliette had retired to their suite, both of them exhausted and emotional. The Indonesians seemed to be treating the whole thing as part of their scheduled activity. They sat in front of the fire, poring over the menu for dinner.

Ethan excused himself and went to his room to take a call from his Sydney office.

Clark in Sydney had bad tidings. The minister for the Interior had gone back on his word to consider Magna-Corp's offer before going public. Turtle Island was now officially on the market.

He sat down in the armchair and stared into the gas fire. Okay, this was the worst-case scenario, but Magna-Corp had the inside running. Ethan had already spent a month on the tender. He was way ahead of the competition. And he had access to all the information and reports Magnus had compiled twenty years ago.

Information that his father would also have on file.

Ethan leaned back in his chair and put his hands behind his head. He couldn't let Magnus and the team down. He would leave soon. After showering he'd go see if Magnus had emerged. He had only a short time to try to persuade his boss to give Summerhill another chance. To help Lucy find out what the hell was going on with Tom.

A short time to spend every waking minute with her, reassuring her, making love to her.

It was cozy by the fire. His last thoughts before he drifted off to sleep were of Lucy looking around at her embattled heritage with such heartache on her face, and then grinning like a naughty child as she wrung the mud from her hair.

Lucy woke him an hour later. She had filled her bath with bubbles, too many bubbles, and wanted to share….

An hour or two later, her stomach gurgled with hunger—or motion sickness. "I'll make us a sandwich."

She tidied the rumpled bed around his drowsy form, doubting he would be awake by the time she got back with the food.

On the way downstairs, her smile faded with each step. She wondered at how torn she felt. On the one hand, she was infused with the well-being that making love with Ethan brought. On the other, she had a heavy heart. Even after a fun-filled hour of giggling and making an unholy mess of her bathroom and then her bed, she felt a weird sense of loss.

His office had called. He hadn't said anything about it, but it was a reminder that he had a whole other life out there, one she wasn't part of. She had to get used to the idea that this little sojourn would soon be over and life would get back to normal.

Lucy wondered if she could ever feel normal again.

Somehow in the last week, her whole perception of herself had undergone radical surgery. She did have something to offer. Instead of letting Tom make all the decisions and ride roughshod over her, she had to persuade him that his half sister had half a brain and wasn't entirely the ditz he thought she was. Ethan built her up, made her feel smart and sexy, not clumsy and stupid. She felt as if she mattered, even knowing he would not be around for much longer.

And that was killing her. She wanted him around, for a long time. Maybe forever. She was falling hopelessly in love.

"And we all know what that means," she murmured to the stag's head at the bottom of the stairs. She had to tell someone, but wasn't quite masochistic enough to tell the man himself. "That means the next thing I hear will be the sound of his running feet."

Well, hell! Nothing was forever. He was here now. He'd promised to help. No point getting down about things she couldn't change.

Forcing a lighter step, she heaped bread and bags of salad vegetables and cheese onto the kitchen counter. She had barely begun when Tom walked in, looking dirty and pale.

Lucy smiled and offered to make him a sandwich. "How's the wrist?"

He held up his plastered limb. "Hellish sore. How was Magnus?"

She shrugged. "By the time Ethan and I got back, they'd gone up to their room." She explained they'd been riding, checking out the stock.

"God," Tom groaned, sitting at the big kauri-wood table, "I have royally screwed up, haven't I?"

"Could have been worse," Lucy told him lightly. He looked so beaten.

"I think we have to face the fact that there will be some changes around here." He examined the plaster cast morosely.

"That's not necessarily a bad thing, is it?" Lucy was thinking of the badly maintained Jeeps, the chef who kept calling in sick, the hunting guide who disregarded a weather report and put lives in danger. The firearms cabinet…

"Tom. I need to talk to you about a couple of things."

He sighed heavily. "Can't it wait? I'm beat."

She ignored that and placed his sandwich beside him. "John Hogan came to see me yesterday. He got his judgment and we have a month to pay or he's starting proceedings for real."

Tom closed his eyes.

"How can things be so bad, we can't even pay an old family friend what we owe him?"

"Everything's gone to hell. Everything I touch."

Lucy, with her back to him, raised her eyes heavenwards. Self-pity was not going to solve anything. "That's not all. I had a visit from a detective. You didn't report the car stolen, or what I told you about Joseph Dunn. Just what's that about?"

Tom slumped. His cast hit the table with a thump. Alarmed, she forgot her sandwich and sat beside him, her hand on his shoulder. "Please talk to me, Tom."

He took a deep breath. "I owe Dunn some money."

Ethan was right. "How much?"

He slumped even farther. It would not have surprised Lucy if he shed tears, he was so down. "How much, Tom?"

He swallowed. "Thousands." It was almost a whisper.

Lucy stared at him, her stomach churning with nerves. There was a long and tense pause. "Your car was found at the scene of an arson. The police want to know whether you had anything to do with it. Did you?"

"I swear. No way, Lucy."

"Ethan thinks Joseph Dunn might be setting you up. Making it look like you were there."

"I wouldn't put it past him. He's a nasty piece of work."

"You have to go see the police. First thing. Tell them about him."

"I will."

He stared down at his untouched sandwich for a long time. "I've let you down. Let everyone down."

She rubbed his shoulder. She might be angry and bewildered but he was family, her only family, and that mattered.

"I never meant for any of this to happen," he was saying.

And then, the dam broke and words just flowed out of him. She stared at his face, disbelieving, and listened while he told a tale so harrowing, she could never have imagined it. How he'd gambled his way into debt. Owed money all over town. How it had been the reason for his marriage break-up shortly before their father had had his stroke.

How he had remortgaged part of their property.

Lucy struggled to take it all in. She reeled with each revelation as if they were blows. He had single-handedly gambled them into debt. To think that he could remortgage a family business and farm that had been theirs for generations.

Fear crawled around her neck. She jumped to her feet and moved quickly to the huge chest against the wall, rummaging through the drawers.

"What are you doing?"

She returned to the table, empty-handed and agitated. "I remember Mum used to stash a pack of cigarettes in there somewhere. I've never wanted to start, but I do right now."

Tom's eyes slid away, but not before she noticed the disparaging look he got whenever her mother was mentioned.

"You never liked my mother, did you?"

He shrugged. "No staying power," he drawled, encompassing her in a sweep of a glance that seemed to imply she was of similar ilk.

"And that's the killer, isn't it?" She leaned forward, her face close to his. "You feel you're the rightful heir to Summerhill because you were born first, to Dad's first wife. You hate that he left half to me."

His eyes met hers and he nodded. "That, and the fact that you've hardly been here. Had nothing to do with building up the lodge..."

"Dad never wanted the lodge in the first place," she countered hotly. "You took advantage of his depression to bully him into it. He was a farmer."

Tom wouldn't meet her eyes and she spent the next moments trying to swallow the anger churning inside. Anger wasn't a normal emotion for her. Usually she met the world with a smile, no matter how anguished she felt. If the world didn't smile back, it was time to move on.

Several big breaths later, she felt composed enough to look at him. "You have to get help. Gambling is an addiction. There are people, organizations who can help you."

After a long time, he raised his head. His eyes were tormented. "On the way back from the police station, I'll go see a business broker. I can't see any other way to make the mortgage payments, or stall the liquidators."

Lucy bridled. "There has to be another way. I won't sell."

"If you're going to be stubborn about it, then we'll have to cut it down the middle. Lucy, I've blown it with Magnus."

She shook her head impatiently. She knew the club

was important, but in the last forty-eight hours, it had assumed less importance for her than her other problems. Especially the one tearing her heart up. "Not necessarily. Ethan is going to bat for us with Magnus."

He stared at her and she saw a nasty little slide of understanding in his eyes. "Ethan this, Ethan that. You two seem cozy."

"He wants to help."

Her hackles rose as he scorched her with a look of such contempt. "He knows, doesn't he? You've been shooting your mouth off."

"He found out on his own. And he was with me when the police came. There wasn't much point in denying anything."

A sneer twisted the corner of his mouth. "You just wait, little sister. We'll be off the list, there will be forty thousand acres of Summerhill land on the market, and your champion will be nowhere to be seen." He shook his head in disgust. "I told you to keep away. You're not equipped to deal with business matters."

There it was again, that disdain for her ability. Lack of respect, even though none of this was her fault. The closeness she'd earlier felt toward him drained away like dirty bathwater.

"Maybe you're not equipped to handle maintenance and safety issues."

"I'm not letting the lodge go down," Tom said belligerently. "I've worked too hard, lost too much, to lose it too."

Lucy stood abruptly and loomed over him. "Then you'll have a fight on your hands," she told him grimly. "I'm sure there is a law about a person who defrauds his business partner to pay gambling debts. And like it or not, Tom, I am your business partner."

His eyes widened. Lucy had never spoken to him like that before. She'd always deferred to him. He was so much smarter than her, and she'd felt so guilty over her past indifference.

Not anymore.

Eleven

Lucy tossed and turned all night and woke at dawn. Creeping out of bed so as not to wake Ethan, she made instant coffee and curled up on the armchair beside the big window, opening the drapes just a sliver.

How she wished to be able to enjoy their first morning waking together. Who knew how many more they'd have?

He'd been asleep when she'd returned from the kitchen last night. She'd snuggled up close, taking comfort from his inert warmth. Pretending he'd be there forever. Trying to erase Tom's contempt and the horror of her financial situation.

What was she worth? What was her value? Not in monetary terms, but in purpose. Tom had been stupid, but she had to accept some responsibility. How different things might have been if she had given instead of always taking. As if taking were her right and there was no effort required on her part to sustain this land of hers.

She sat there in a fearful misery for an hour before Ethan woke. Tousled, naked, a sleepy smile on his wicked lips, he brought a little burst of hope to her heart.

He was starving, so Lucy phoned the kitchen and cajoled a light breakfast. She crawled back into bed and told him the whole story of her conversation with Tom last night.

"How could he remortgage without your consent?" he demanded.

"He had power of attorney for Dad. After the stroke, Dad was deemed to be incapable."

"You have to find out how much and how immediate the debt is," he told her brusquely.

Lucy didn't miss the inflection on *you*. It was an unwelcome reminder that their short interlude was drawing to a close.

"Trouble is," he continued, "there are unlikely to be any records of gambling debts. I'll go see Magnus first thing and try to stall his decision for a bit. You don't want Tom flying off the handle and making rash decisions."

Room service arrived with their breakfast and Ethan disappeared into the bathroom to dress. Lucy poured coffee for herself. Ethan liked tea in the mornings. A piece of useless information she would hold in her heart.

How little she knew of him. How was it possible to feel so much so quickly, with as much room for growth as a root-bound potted plant? She wondered if in ten years, she would recall that little detail: I once fell in love with a man who liked to drink tea in the mornings.

He returned from the bathroom in pants and with his shirt unbuttoned, and sat down opposite her. She offered the teapot, waiting for him to raise his cup. He seemed subdued. "I have to get back to Sydney." His eyes glided to her face. "Tomorrow."

Lucy's heart sank. The teapot stilled in midair. So soon....

He pushed his cup toward her. "There's a problem." He looked straight at her then. "I had hoped for a few more days."

She began to pour, feeling a tremble threaten her fingers. "Work's important," she said inanely.

"Will you be all right?"

"'Course." Said lightly, as in "Don't be silly." She set the pot down carefully.

Ethan leaned back, still looking at her. "I have to go. But…"

Lucy blinked. Was that guilt in his eyes? "Can't be helped." The last thing she wanted was to make him feel guilty. None of this was his problem.

"I'll be back—soon as I can—if you want, that is…"

And then you'll go again. And soon, you'll be immersed in your project. And I'll be here, and the calls will come less often. "I hope you get the deal. It's important to you."

"Paramount," Ethan told her. "After this one, a change of direction."

Lucy tried to look interested, but it was hard when she was saying goodbye inside.

"I was thinking of buying some land somewhere. Do you think you could live anywhere else but Summerhill?"

Lucy looked up sharply. He had asked the question in the same breath as he finished the statement, she noted. If she had done that, it would suggest she was breathless, nervous. She tried and failed to imagine Ethan nervous—although she had seen breathless....

She repeated the question in her head. Could she live anywhere else? With you? she wanted to ask. Maybe with you, she answered herself. Her fingers made a mess of toast crumbs on her plate. Was he asking her to go with him?

Her overactive brain then slipped in a worrying new thought. Was he just trying to prepare her for the worst? They hadn't discussed what he had found out in the village. Maybe he was trying to tell her she didn't have a hope in hell of keeping Summerhill anyway. "If I did that, Tom would just carve it up."

Ethan nodded slowly. She could see the sky blue of her robe in his eyes, but beyond that were shadows of regret. The two things she would hate most for him to take away from here were regret and guilt.

"Lucy, I'll be at the end of the phone."

Shame put an edge on her voice. "Don't worry," she insisted. "I told him I'd fight him about selling the land."

"I know you will."

Yes, she thought. You gave me that. A week ago, I wouldn't have fought.

An awful uncomfortable silence ensued as they both pretended to be busy with their breakfast. She darted furtive looks at him across the small table. Can I live with this? With his body every few months and his deep, slow voice on the phone. He will go. And I will visit occasionally. And it won't be more than we are able to give.

Lucy inhaled, making a conscious effort not to clench her jaw. She couldn't take pity from him. She did not want sacrifices and ultimatums. She looked up to see him watching her, concern darkening his eyes.

He exhaled noisily. "Dammit! I'll stay…"

Her whole body tensed. She would not be a liability. His liability. Making a snap decision, she rose abruptly. There was one way she knew of to shut a man up before he said something that could not be reversed.

Her body would succor them both. A fist of desire tightened in her stomach. It was desperate and consuming, and she saw that he recognised it. Perhaps awash with his unwanted guilt, he approved of it.

This is what I can give, and it *is* heartfelt, and it doesn't need words.

He rose, too, as she reached for him. They came together at the edge of the table and her hands were at his belt, tugging him toward the bed. As they lurched together, he cupped her face and kissed her deeply.

Lucy sighed into his mouth, overcome by a mindless lust. She pushed the shirt off his shoulders. Biceps bunched and rippled under her eager strokes. She dug her nails into his flat belly, then scraped gently down. Impatient to tear those pants off, loving the feel of taut and supple skin and his earthy, morning-male scent.

She strove to shrink his focus to nothing but sensation. When he was far away, she wanted him to remember this—how she made him feel. No guilt to taint his memory. She wanted a physical, tangible memory of her to stay inside him. She wanted to *be* inside him.

Long, taut and muscular, his skin taunted her fingertips. Her nerve endings hummed with the anticipation of having everything she wanted right here in front of her, drowning in need.

The lower she went, the more still he became, but she heard the blood rushing through his veins. Down, she pushed at his trousers and briefs, bending her knees. Up, her hands smoothed around his buttocks, kneading the clenched muscles. His thighs strained like tree trunks, but he quivered when she took him in her hands. She made one long firm stroke from his heated curved underside up the length of him, loving the tensile resistance and the way he strained toward her. Her fingertips swept over the thick tip of him. His groan swept from his fingers into her mind as his hands landed lightly on her head.

She felt the heat flooding into him, the satiny skin tight and hot, scorching a trail to her heart.

Ethan couldn't watch when he saw her perfect lips part and close around him. Too erotic. With the unmanageable hang-up he had about her mouth, he wouldn't last ten seconds if he watched.

The need to thrust screamed through him. He braced his thighs, confident in his strength, and was shocked to find himself trembling.

He knew what she was doing. Once again, deflecting attention away from her problems, her desolation by using her impressive arsenal. Charm, kissing, sex. He'd learned that about her.

He groaned as she took him deeper. Hell of a way to cope.

But she was tough enough to cope with Tom, even if she didn't know that yet, and Ethan fully intended to back her up all the way.

Just not in person right now. And he felt bad about that.

He felt terrible about that.

More—too much! He wanted her beautiful mouth on his. Whispering her name, he stroked through her hair down to her face and coaxed her up. She met his lips with her own when he dipped his head. Something brimmed in her eyes, abstract and sad, but before he could wonder, worry, he was taken over by her kiss, distracted by the feel of her body against his. He molded her body close and felt the cool slide of his wet erection against her robe-covered belly. The blue of her eyes now smoked up into something more immediate.

She pressed forward into him, her spine arched. He slipped the loose knot of her robe so that it hung down, still covering her breasts. Mesmerized by the luster of her skin against the cool blue of the fabric, he reached out and touched her through the robe. She took a deep breath in, so her chest rose and rose. The silky fabric slid under his fingers and over her skin with a liquid sensuality that nevertheless dried his throat like chalk.

Around and around in little circles, under and over, slipping and sliding like an ice cube melting. Her breath stopped when the material sighed over the hard tips of her breasts. His throat closed when she let her head loll back, his whispered name trickling out through her parted lips.

It was an age before she reached for another breath. As he took his silken touch lower, he drew the robe slowly down her arms. Where the fabric touched, his mouth followed. Her marble skin quivered and tightened. He rubbed and licked and kissed his way right down to her toes, then discarded the robe and started up again. Her sweet musky smell broke over him, making him sweat with greed. With one arm wrapped around her to support her trembling legs, his mouth and fingers took what he needed and gave her the release she craved.

As if he'd turned a switch, her every muscle seized. On and on, it screeched and ripped through her, that fine edge between pleasure and pain not just blurred but

shattered like a windscreen. Holding her together by the
tips of her fingernails, by the edge of her teeth. When
his hands began to soothe the cramped muscles in the
backs of her legs, she flopped back onto the bed, quak-
ing. She had kissed the sky with his name on her lips.
But now—in a minute when she got her breath—she
was filled with another burn. Aggravated by aftershocks
of such sweetness, she needed his abrasive invading
presence inside her. Needed to be stretched, filled,
grounded.

With arms that felt like jelly, she gripped his shoulders and hauled him up over her. With a mouth that
wanted to sob with the ecstasy that streamed through
every cell, every particle that made her whole, she
crooned her wish into his ear, then kissed him. Felt his
smile against her lips and tasted herself and his need.

There was nothing more ragingly erotic than a
woman who talked dirty, especially when it filtered out
through the lips of an angel.

He wanted to immerse himself, to feel her moving,
flowing under and around him. Their kiss promised
pleasure to come, and an exchange of tenderness that
bewildered him. Too much emotion. He broke off the
kiss and nuzzled her throat. Dangerous, maybe life-
altering emotion.

He reached toward the depleted box of condoms
on her bedside table where they had been since last
night. Quickly sheathing himself, he lay back over
her, sinking into her kiss again. His hands moved,
inch by inch up her forearms, entwining her fingers
in his.

Face-to-face, bodies pressed together, his hips
hunched into the cradle of hers. He eased into her and

in the brightening morning light, watched her eyes fill with warmth, spiced with danger.

Slow and deep. Sweat broke out on his forehead and he nipped and nuzzled her mouth, swallowing her labored little breaths. Her hips rocked and rolled, and he felt himself so deep, so lushly gloved. The humming in his ears sounded like an old refrigerator, surging and retreating and vibrating.

She rocked and squeezed and her inner thighs gripped him in velvet welcome. The blood screamed through his every vein, every artery. He felt again the change in her body temperature and an intimate swelling. Heard the desperate sighs that signaled her focus. Her fingers were locked onto his and she seemed to gather for a last great push. Ethan tensed and thrust deep.

Lucy shattered. Incoherent baby words rushed out of her mouth as her head thrashed from side to side. He heard his name, felt her contractions dissolve him into a heavy, drenching mist of pure pleasure.

Afterward she lay on her side but cuddled in close. Her drawn-up knees were jammed into his gut and she held him tightly.

"I really love that thing you do," he murmured into her hair.

"What thing?"

"After you come. All elbows and knees and head, like you're trying to climb right inside my rib cage."

He felt her mouth move against his throat. "Do I? Sorry."

Ethan increased the pressure of his arms, holding her closer. "I love it. It's what it's all about, isn't it?"

He listened to her breathing pan out and deepen. He bet she'd gotten little sleep last night after Tom's bombshell.

He pressed his lips to the top of her head, feeling little peace himself. Or eagerness to get back to work. Or even self-satisfaction after the best sex of his life.

She was warm and smelled sexy. For a moment, his chest expanded so completely, his arms were compelled to cuddle her closer. Then a hollow feeling deflated him.

First things first. Get Turtle Island started. Land the deal.

Lousy timing, when everything was crashing around her ears. Could he stall, just for a couple of days? On the other hand, he had read the economy reports. Could the islanders afford to alienate MagnaCorp?

Ethan craned his neck to look at the curve of Lucy's cheek, the shadows her lashes made on her pale skin.

Be patient, stick to the plan and in a couple of short years—less—he could relax, kick back, contemplate the future. Maybe with Lucy in it—if she still wanted him.

Contemplate Lucy.

Her knees scraped down his body slowly and now there was no impediment between them. She nestled in closer with a contented sigh. His heart swelled again, perplexing him. So much more intimacy than ever before.

Contemplate love. Loving Lucy.

Ethan squeezed his eyes shut, then snapped them open again.

Lucy donned raincoat and gum boots and walked down to clean out the stables. Their stablehand had been cut off by the flood yesterday and she couldn't return the horses to the stable until the stalls had been cleared.

She found the smell of sodden slimy straw and mud quite suited her mood. Rank and festering.

Lucy was tired of people she cared about being indifferent toward her. She must deserve it, because that was all she had ever inspired in people—at least the people she wanted love from. Basically, she wasn't lovable. Had never been, starting from the day her mother had left.

Sweep, sweep. She was working up a sweat here.

There was something about her that meant she would never be number one. She would always be part-time, long-distance, ditzy, nice little Lucy.

Her pique was unreasonable. She could no more expect him to give up his job, his life than he could expect her to walk away from her birthright. She leaned on her broom, panting with exertion and frustration. *If* that is what he had been referring to.

Although if Tom had his way, her birthright would be chopped up and flushed away. And what would she be left with then?

What she'd always had. Nothing. Nobody. And nowhere to run. She bent her back to her work and was vigorous about it.

What were the options? The most logical and probable: stay here and battle Tom's obstinacy, possibly his enemies and definitely his demons, while trying somehow to turn Summerhill from a debt-ridden, badly-run lodge and neglected farm, into—what? Did she even have any idea?

Or she could jump on the nearest plane and fly off to—Paris? Prague?—though the language would be a problem and languages were *so* not her forte. Didn't matter where. It had always worked for her in the past. Until her father had gotten sick and the vein of money had become plugged.

But—she pulled her hat off, overheating. Maybe

Ethan loved her, or could grow to love her. He gave her something. Hope. With him, anything seemed possible. She felt smart, not dumb. She had good ideas. And perhaps now a little belief in herself.

Her mind darted about like a blind moth.

What would he do if she told him, right now, she loved him? Would he run just as everyone she had ever cared for had? Could she ever be happy with only a part of him?

A familiar figure slopped across the yard outside the stables. The stablehand had arrived. She watched him approach but was so deep in thought, she didn't really register she was no longer alone.

He stopped and they looked at each other, then he reached out for the broom. "Jeez," he said, wheezing a little. "We've been in drought for three years and now this. It's all or nothing, eh?"

He tugged the broom from her grasp and began sweeping. Lucy looked after him, his words seeping through the fetid smell of the stable.

All or nothing. Why did it have to be? She could eat two pieces of the pie, couldn't she? Instead of the whole thing or none at all.

She started for the house before she lost her nerve. Maybe the fermenting straw had addled her brain, but she was going to walk into the house and tell him she was in love with him. She was going to face the issue instead of running. This was life. There was no fairy-tale family life, no loving, indulgent parents. Just Lucy and her equal love for Summerhill land and for Ethan Rae.

Ethan took the stairs two at a time, fuelled by anger, shame—and relief. In his room, he tossed his bag onto the bed and began to fill it. Relief? Because there was no choice to be made now. Everything was back to normal.

Acid rose in his throat like the burn of Tom's words.

Ethan and Magnus had been in the conference facility for half an hour before Tom burst in. Magnus's overriding concern was safety—his wife had let slip about the afternoon weather report Tom had chosen to ignore.

"Can't control the weather," Tom had snapped, shooting a venomous look at Ethan. He obviously thought Lucy had blabbed.

Poor sap. His back was against the wall. Unwittingly, Magnus built the fire, stoked it, till Tom felt he had no option but to blame Lucy for everything.

"Lady Luck turns her back sometimes, Magnus," Tom had wheedled. "It's cyclical. You're a businessman. You know that."

"Not good enough, son. A big part of your business is safety." Magnus paused, and hammered home the second nail in Lucy's coffin. "If Lucy hadn't remembered that hut, we'd still be out there now."

Now Ethan yanked savagely on the zip of the suit compartment of his bag and heard the door open. He threw Lucy an icy look when she entered his room but forced himself to continue with his mental checklist. Shirt, underwear, toiletries—he was nearly done. His movements were quick and efficient but tension wired his jaw and stretched his spine into a hostile rod.

From the corner of his eye, he saw her hover in the doorway, her black jeans stained and tucked into long woolly socks that dropped bits of plant matter onto the floor. She looked flushed and rumpled.

"What are you doing?" she asked quietly, twisting her hands together in front of her.

His hands crushed the clothing down, then he hauled on the zip. Lucy flinched at the scraping thud of the bag hitting the floor. He continued to pretend to ignore her, moving to the table to organize his laptop and briefcase.

"You really had me going," he muttered after an age.

"Wh-what do you mean?"

"Should have chosen your accomplice with more care." Bitterness scoured his throat. Tom's sneering face flashed past his eyes. "Your brother loused it up for you."

Without looking at her, Ethan sensed her cringe with foreboding. Not his problem. Laptop snapped shut, papers stacked, briefcase closed. "If he'd just been patient…but Tom couldn't leave it alone. He burst in, ranting and raving about how he knew we were cutting him loose. How, because of *our* pillow talk, Magnus knew about the court case, the gambling, the debt, the shady associates." He smiled grimly at his watch, slapped his pockets. "Funny thing was, I hadn't told Magnus any of that."

Before Tom's intrusion, Ethan had secured a stay in the decision about Summerhill's place on the Global List. He'd also mentioned that Lucy had some good ideas that deserved to be given a chance. In an effort to calm Tom, Magnus suggested he take a leaf out of his sister's book.

A red rag to a bull…

The elderly, respected businessman was unprepared for Tom's insults, the final one: that his precious club was a highfalutin bag of hot air that Summerhill could manage without. Magnus had stormed out, calling loudly to his wife to get her things.

Ethan laid the briefcase and laptop on top of his bag and scooped up his jacket. Lucy stood silent. Not wanting to, knowing he shouldn't, he raked his eyes over her face. Not just milky-pale now, a much more deathly hue. Her eyes were anguished; those perfect lips parted slightly.

Ethan blinked and looked away, pushing his arms into the sleeves of his jacket. Maybe he wasn't quite as cold, as pitiless as his sense of justice demanded. Seeing her lips tremble would only haunt him later.

"And then he told me about your carefully orchestrated plan. How you agreed to do *anything* for Summerhill, even prostitute yourself to snag a rich husband."

"What?" Her voice was faint. "No."

He turned his back and walked to the window. The lush green of freshly saturated pasture was soothing, but he'd need a whole universe of it to forget Tom's fleshy lips spitting out the truth. According to him, his sister might not have much in the brain department, but she was as skilled as her worthless mother when it came to playing men—and Ethan had been played like a flute.

Did you think you were the first? Tom had taunted. *You were just rich and single and about thirty years younger than her usual smorgasbord. Ask her why she came home.*

"You told him you would seduce me," Ethan muttered, "get me—and therefore Magnus—on side. I was your ticket to saving your land."

"No."

Ethan turned to her, glowering. "Can you deny it?"

Her lips moved soundlessly. Something awful—a realization—limped across her face. Then guilt. Somehow, without moving a muscle she seemed to shrink. His heart lurched even lower, his jaw clamped even tighter.

"It was a joke," she whispered. "The first night we met. I was fooling around."

"Very funny." He walked to his luggage, took the briefcase and laptop in one hand and shouldered the big bag.

Damn those trembling lips. He had to get out of here. There was a deal to clinch. He should have known better than to mess with emotions while there was work to do.

An image of his father, smiling benevolently at a twenty-something busty blonde danced in his mind. That one had lasted two or three years but the result was the same. When it ended, she still took his father to the cleaners.

Ask her why she came home…

She was frozen to the spot.

He glared down at her. "Why *did* you come home, Lucy?"

Her shoulders jerked. If she was surprised about anything, it was the way he sounded. She had come to love his voice. Deep and smooth as caramel.

She wanted to cover her ears. He was so harsh, so bitingly cold. This was the man she was about to confess her love for?

"The stroke." Her voice wavered. She made an effort. "Dad's stroke." Firmer.

He stared at her face for a long moment. "Wasn't it because Tom stopped the party fund?"

Lucy exhaled noisily, opened her mouth, but he cut her off. Disdain twisted his mouth and he clucked his tongue. "Such low expectations, Lucy. I'm wealthy but hardly in the league of some of the men you entice here. And you'd have to wait a while to inherit."

She just shook her head miserably. She knew she should defend herself. But her words would bounce off that rigid form, the pitiless glitter in his eyes. What had she ever done or said that made a difference to anyone before?

"I had wondered if you were a common gold digger from the first. In your position, it wouldn't be surprising and you were quite open with your charming little quips about wanting a rich husband."

She shook her head miserably. "Ethan, if you can believe that…" Her voice sounded about a hundred years old to her ears.

"I thought you were different. Thought I was a good judge of character—something I will have to reevaluate."

His hands gripped his luggage tightly. He straightened. "Your big miscalculation was, I despise women like you. You must have seen that from the get-go."

Lucy exhaled, a long ragged breath. "Walk away then." Her shoulders jerked in another pitiful excuse for a shrug. "It's easiest."

He jerked his chin toward the table. "My check for the accommodation."

Lucy's eyes followed the movement and stayed there. She heard but didn't watch, knew well enough the sight of a door close in her face. She stared blindly at the table, amazed that there was no pain. Just a constriction in her chest, like the old, familiar iron lung had taken up residency. Without making a conscious decision, her legs took her over to the table. The check lay there, flat, unfeeling.

That was something else she knew well. A check, if not to make you feel better, then to keep you quiet until the next time something rose up and lodged in your throat so you made a fuss about it. Till someone noticed and looked at you, sighed a long-suffering sigh and wrote out another check.

Outside, the van moved off down the driveway, crunching on the gravel. She hadn't even said goodbye to Juliette.

Twelve

Ethan walked out of the elevator on the ninth floor to the sharp sound of applause. Dog-tired, bemused, he was surrounded by smiling colleagues shaking his hand, slapping his back. The small throng dispersed when Clark approached with a grin as wide as the Grand Canyon. "We got the fax half an hour ago. You did it!"

Clark led him to the anteroom of Magnus's office, still pumping his hand heartily. Even the very proper Beryce, Magnus's PA for twenty years, was rising, smiling, ushering them through the door into the office.

Where was the relief, he wondered as he was enveloped in a bear hug? The triumph? The satisfaction that accompanied revenge?

His boss sloshed overgenerous slugs of cognac into glasses, serving the three of them, lighting their cigars. The excited flow of words between the other two men never faltered. They toasted each other and sat.

"Holy cow, boy! It's the deal of the century, even though it cost me both arms and both legs."

Ethan listened, drank, smoked and chastised himself for his lack of enthusiasm.

"When can you get started?"

He swallowed the burning liquid and squinted through a heavy haze of smoke. "You like the islands, Clark?" he asked finally. "Pack enough for a couple of years."

He drained his glass and watched the delight fade on his mentor's face.

Hours later, fuzzy-headed from unaccustomed afternoon drinking, he walked into his harbor-side apartment, tossed his jacket over a chair and called his father in Perth. "How you doing?"

"What?"

Ethan was ashamed at the astonishment in Jackson Rae's voice. His usual inquiries were about work, or the latest squeeze. They exchanged stilted pleasantries then Ethan took a deep breath. "You're out of the picture for Turtle Island."

There was a long pause. "How did you know I bid?"

"Didn't. I guessed you would."

"Should have known you wouldn't call just to say gidday."

Ethan knew he deserved that. In the silence that followed, he racked his brain to come up with something to soften the blow. He had a lot to learn about building bridges. But you had to start somewhere. "I'm—sorry."

"Must have been a hell of a deal," his father growled.

"It was. I've resigned," he added.

There was another lengthy pause. "You and that old reprobate fallen out?"

"Parted on excellent terms." A throb in his temple reminded him of the depleted level of liquid left in the brandy bottle. They had parted close. Maudlin close.

"What will you do? There is a place for you here."

Ethan smiled at the lightning-quick offer. "Thanks but no, Dad." He heard his father's breath catch. He probably hadn't called him Dad since he'd been a young boy. At school, he was "sir." On his rare home visits, he used "Father," and on his few-and-far-between phone calls he usually just announced, "It's Ethan," to preclude having to use a title. "I'm going to farm."

"Farm? But don't you remember...? You can't rewrite history, son."

Ethan smiled into the phone. "I'm going to try."

The smooth hum of the Nissan wasn't a bit like the Alfa's deeper, frothy growl. She supposed she would miss her status symbol but she'd only had it a few months. Tom had grumbled, but Lucy insisted it would add class to the operation. She wasn't aware back then of how much financial trouble they were in.

A sign flashed by indicating the turn-off for the inland route to the mountains. Why was she not driving to the airport? The smart black briefcase on the passenger seat positively groaned with ready money. Enough to live on for a good while, she considered.

Lucy checked the rearview mirror and indicated a lane change. She noticed the same line by her mouth she had seen that morning, making up. The iron band around her torso seemed to tighten.

Damn him. Wrinkles. A pain around the heart. A ruby-red suit. *I'd love to see you in red.*

But up ahead the morning sun glistened off a jagged jawline of fresh-coated mountains. She forced the sadness away. If she gave in to it, she had better be prepared to spend the rest of her life running. And if thinking of a way to save her land kept her from giving in to the heartbreak that would shatter her, that was as good an excuse as any in a life full of excuses.

By the time she parked outside the lodge and marched up to the door of Tom's office, she was resolute. Not nice, malleable little Lucy now. She knew she was strong. Ethan had given her that, if nothing else.

For the last two weeks, Tom had been subdued and surprisingly receptive to her suggestions. He felt guilty about the debts and his part in Ethan's departure, for which he had confessed all and apologized repeatedly. She understood better why Ethan had run.

That didn't make it any easier to bear.

Tom had better appreciate her efforts today. She'd raised enough to cover their creditors and Tom's personal gambling debt—assuming he had disclosed everything. But they would have to generate a lot more income to cover the payments for the part-mortgage he had taken out against the property.

Resolute maybe, but she still crossed the fingers of her free hand.

Her heels clicked across the wooden floor, quick and sharp. And stopped dead.

Ethan Rae sat across from Tom, the big kauri-wood desk between them. Her heart seemed to squeeze and crumple. A kaleidoscope of frantic thoughts whirled through her brain.

Her eyes drank him in. God, he looked good. Lucy had tried to forget his features, his commanding presence. Powerful. Alert and primed for success. Without doubts.

She would not be moved by the warm approval that

leapt into his eyes as they roved over her body. The suit wasn't for him.

She deliberately turned her head without acknowledging him. "I thought we had an appointment."

"Ethan surprised me. Want some coffee?"

Lucy walked toward them on legs that felt like glass. A fierce compulsion to run far and fast tangled up the words in her throat. Before her nerve fled, she placed the briefcase on the corner of the desk and drew out a sheaf of papers.

"There is enough there to clear all our debt, except for the mortgage."

Tom took the papers she offered. "You sold the apartment?" His voice was incredulous. He held up the valuation on the apartment.

"The auction's next week." She didn't divulge the estate agent's warning that an urgent auction rarely reached the reserve. "I sold the car and the painting."

Had Ethan jerked in surprise then? She recalled his interest in the valuable gift from her father. So what? She forced her attention back to her brother.

She had never seen Tom really surprised. His fleshy mouth opened and closed spasmodically.

"God, Luce, this is—stunning."

"There's more." She indicated the large white envelope under the checks. Tom drew out the information on Gamblers Anonymous, flushing deeply. The appointment card was stapled to the front. Ten o'clock next Thursday morning. She would be accompanying him. "And I went to see the police. They're looking into Joseph Dunn. They know him well."

Her hands were empty now. She raised her chin and walked to the window. Minutes ticked by and she knew, by the tightening of her pores, that Ethan's eyes bored into her back. This was her biggest test. Get the business out of the way and escape.

But why was he here? More accusations? Maybe an apology…but that was silly. Why, then, would he be meeting with Tom?

She did not turn around until she heard Tom's exhalation. Wound as tight as a spring, she knew to look at Ethan would unravel her. Lucy acknowledged she would have to go through the pain of losing him one day, but not here, not now and certainly not with him present.

Her brother's eyes shone as he looked up at her. "I don't know what to say. This is amazing." Tom shifted in his chair and Lucy didn't miss the quick conspiratorial look that passed between the two men.

She walked back over to his desk and sat. "We'd be debt-free, Tom, except for the mortgage. So you see, we don't need the club." Of their own accord, her eyes flicked disdainfully to the man at her left. "And we don't need to sell the land."

Tom fidgeted with his pen and shuffled papers. "Ah. Well, that's why Ethan is here. He's come up with a very interesting business proposition."

A shard of ice slipped through the band of steel around her chest. A business proposition? Was he trying to buy their land? He knew their backs were against the wall. He also knew that if he threw money at Tom…

"It's a lease, Lucy," Tom went on. "If Ethan were to lease the arable land from us, it would mean he pays us a lump sum up front and a yearly rent for whatever term we decide on."

"But—we don't need to sell…"

"Not sell. Lease. He'd be like a tenant."

The shard of ice hurtled around in a flyaway panic

that even the tight band around her chest could not contain. It would be impossible to conduct a business relationship with Ethan Rae. Not when she felt the way she did about him. Not when he'd made it brutally clear what his opinion of her was.

She glanced at him briefly, fearfully. "I don't understand."

"Ethan wants to farm. He would set up the farm at his own expense."

Lucy felt stupid and covered it up with a scowl. "No. It's McKinlay land."

Ethan cleared his throat, startling her. "Tom, would you mind?"

Panic gripped her. Don't leave me alone with him, she implored Tom with her eyes. But he was rising, nodding, closing the door behind him.

Silence engulfed the room like a cloud. Lucy tried to hold all that she was feeling in her hands, clasped in a death grip in her lap.

Ethan lounged three feet away, long legs stretched out in front of him. Finally, he spoke. "A lease means that the land is still yours and Tom's, Lucy. You are the legal owners. I would just be borrowing it for whatever period you decide. Two years, ten, twenty…"

She inhaled—as much as possible with her ribs in an iron corset. Since talking was beyond her, she might as well listen.

"The initial lump sum could get rid of your debt."

She flicked a hand at the papers on the desk and felt his eyes on her.

"You are incredible." His voice had altered, from businesslike to soft. "Your family doesn't deserve you."

A hard little knot of hurt made her want to cut. "What

would you know of family? You won't even forgive
your father."

The guilt she felt at that remark irked her even more.
He'd hurt her, dammit. She was sick of sheathing her
claws. Turning in her seat, she faced him. "In fact,
you're not a very forgiving man, are you Ethan? I don't
think I'd like you as a business partner or tenant or
whatever it is you're talking about."

He had been looking at the desk in front of him, but
now he faced her. He was hunched back in his seat with
his hands in his pockets. After a lengthy pause, he spoke.
"Unlike your father, you now have a mortgage to fur-
nish. This way, you will get an income from the land."

Lucy sighed. Confusion—and curiosity—retracted
her claws. "So what do you get out of it?"

"The profits from what I produce. I pay for everything—stock, feed, fertilizer. And I keep the profits."

"What about the lodge?"

"Not affected in any way. The lease would only cover
the productive farming land. You and Tom would continue to run the lodge as you are now."

She was not looking at him but heard the smile in his
voice. "Well, maybe not quite as you are now, I hope."

Lucy didn't smile in return.

"You could implement some of your very good ideas
for the lodge. Once the financial pressure is off, Lucy,
anything is possible."

"Who would look after the farm?" Her voice was
faint. It was inconceivable to her that she would be
sharing this part of the world with this man. She really
would have to run.

"Me."

Panic sharpened her tone. "From Sydney? Or Turtle…Tortoise Island or whatever it is?"

He shook his head.

She was tired of guessing. "You're a businessman, not a farmer," she informed him impatiently.

"Told you I wanted to farm one day."

"One day!" She jumped to her feet. "What about your job? Your big important deal?" She only allowed him a heartbeat or two before continuing. "Thanks for the offer, but don't worry about us. We'll manage."

"I resigned," he told her quietly, looking up at her.

Her heart gave a jolt. Flooded her with something— hope? It slopped against the iron band around her chest.

She pushed it down.

His eyes caressed her face. His expression rocked her—all regret and apology. Another wave of confusion swept her. How different he looked and sounded from the icy stranger of a week ago. How could he hate her, hurt her like that and yet expect to work alongside her? Was it to humiliate her? Her eyes and throat ached with unshed tears. Please go and let me cry in peace, she begged silently, looking down at her shoes.

"Lucy, I'm sorry."

She pursed her lips to quell that damn hope that seemed to swell inside again. His voice was dangerous, reminded her of what they'd shared—and lost.

"Truly sorry." He rose, took two steps until he stood in front of her. His aftershave, tangy and fresh, wafted to her and she breathed it in on a slow careful inhalation.

"I should never have believed Tom and gone off half-cocked."

Her fingers curled into fists by her sides.

"You weren't in the plan, and you know me. I never deviate from the plan." He paused again, but she still couldn't trust herself to speak.

Undaunted by her silence, he continued. "That last day, making love to you, I was *this* close to saying to hell with the job. *This* close to saying I'm not leaving you while everything is crashing around your ears. That scared the daylights out of me."

Lucy heard the snap of his fingers and then her heart beating. Strong, steady, resonant.

"When Tom said what he did, it was a lifeline. I grabbed it and ran."

She could not bring herself to look at him yet, but she had to know. "Wh-what changed your mind?"

He paused. "I was doing the same thing I'd done all my working life. Trying to prove I was better at it than Dad. And this deal—Turtle Island—it was the biggie. The one that would really kick him in the guts because of his history with it."

Lucy did look up at him then. His eyes glowed with regret. "All through this last week, I've thought only of you. Your loyalty and compassion, and how you've learned to cope. Your strength and your wonderful bond with this land. Made my goals seem petty and mean." His voice softened. "And I was missing you bad and feeling like a heel because I'd run out on you, accusing you of something I knew you weren't and could never be."

He flexed and curled his hands. "I was a coward, Lucy. Easier to walk away, close a deal, blame you for something you didn't do, than face the fact that I'm in love with you."

Lucy's heart stopped. She dug her nails into her palms to feel the scrape of something real. Forced her scurrying mind to slow, to comprehend. He loved her? Hope reared up again.

"Make me a better man, Lucy." His smooth, dark voice curled around her, at once soothing and agitating.

"Give me some of that compassion and loyalty of yours. I don't want my son not to talk to me for twenty years."

Her heart jerked again. How was it possible to still be standing while racked with so many different emotions?

So she sat down with a plop. "You are a good man, Ethan," she whispered. "You're kind. You know how to get the best out of people. You understand how I feel about Summerhill, and you've helped me to stand and fight and actually believe I can do it."

"You can do it. You have done it." He pointed at the papers on Tom's desk. "But you don't have to do it on your own." He squatted down in front of her and took her hand. "I'm not doing anything for the next fifty years. Let me help you. Let's make this our business, Lucy. Do it with me."

"I—I don't know what to say." She stared down at him, searched his face and found honesty and sincerity.

"Say you accept my apology. Say you love me, too. Say you'll marry me."

Her eyes blurred. When was the killer blow going to come? Things like this didn't happen in real life.

"I was coming to tell you," she blurted, "the other day, before you left, that I love you. That we'd work it out somehow."

He pressed her hand to his lips. "I'm sorry I ruined it. Say it now. And say yes."

She shook her head in wonder. "You would live here with me, without owning a bit of it?"

"You and Summerhill come as a package deal, evidently." They smiled at each other. "Don't care where we live. We could build up on the gorge, if you like."

"No electricity. No water. No access."

"It's what I do, Lucy."

She nodded, eyes shining.

"Anyway," he continued, "I have property all over the world."

"You do?" Her face fell when he nodded. "But then I'd be like a trophy wife."

Ethan threaded his fingers through hers, kissed her hand again. "You own this incredible land. And if you say yes to the lease, soon you will own the best, most productive high-country station in New Zealand."

She looked down into his eyes. There it was: a warmth and reassurance she could bathe in. A respect and admiration hope could flourish in.

He stood, taking her hands and pulling her up. "Say yes, Lucy."

"What am I saying yes to again?" She could almost hear the iron chains around her torso shattering. Hope, love streaked through the ruins, making her giddy.

"Yes, you accept my apology?"

"Yes."

"Yes, you love me, too?"

"Oh, yes!"

"Yes, you'll marry me?"

She hesitated. "*If* you invite your father to the wedding."

He nodded, smiling. "And yes to the lease. I need something to occupy my time while you're off with your trophy wives."

"I suppose I could put my X to that." She sighed.

Ethan moved back a step. "Almost forgot." He took something from his jacket pocket and handed it to her. "For you."

They were tickets of some kind.

"He is a world-renowned expert on learning disabilities. The seminar is in Sydney next month, which gives you time to organize an assessment beforehand."

Really, she was touched, but old habits die hard. She gave a mock sigh. "Oh, Ethan. But there are lots more exciting things to do in Sydney than some boring old—"

He held up his index finger. "We'll make it a brief stopover on the way to our honeymoon." He slid his arms around her waist. "It's time to front up, Lucy. Stop pretending it doesn't exist and doesn't matter."

She rolled her eyes. "Okay then. If you insist."

She put her arms around him, too, laying her head on his chest. She felt oddly quiet, full—cherished. For the first time in a long time.

Through the window, she saw the line of trees, a guard of honor leading to the river. And beyond, the lofty ridges and steep spurs of the far off Alps, wreathed in snow.

She might not have the best business head in the world, but Lucy McKinlay knew a good deal when she saw one.

From *USA TODAY*
bestselling author

Annette
Broadrick

THE MAN
MEANS BUSINESS

(SD #701)

When a business trip suddenly
turns into a passionate affair,
what's a millionaire and
his secretary to do once
they return to the office?

Available this January from Silhouette Desire

If you enjoyed what you just read,
then we've got an offer you can't resist!

Take 2 bestselling love stories FREE!
Plus get a FREE surprise gift!

Clip this page and mail it to Silhouette Reader Service™

IN U.S.A.	**IN CANADA**
3010 Walden Ave.	P.O. Box 609
P.O. Box 1867	Fort Erie, Ontario
Buffalo, N.Y. 14240-1867	L2A 5X3

YES! Please send me 2 free Silhouette Desire® novels and my free surprise gift. After receiving them, if I don't wish to receive anymore, I can return the shipping statement marked cancel. If I don't cancel, I will receive 6 brand-new novels every month, before they're available in stores! In the U.S.A., bill me at the bargain price of $3.80 plus 25¢ shipping and handling per book and applicable sales tax, if any*. In Canada, bill me at the bargain price of $4.47 plus 25¢ shipping and handling per book and applicable taxes**. That's the complete price and a savings of at least 10% off the cover prices—what a great deal! I understand that accepting the 2 free books and gift places me under no obligation ever to buy any books. I can always return a shipment and cancel at any time. Even if I never buy another book from Silhouette, the 2 free books and gift are mine to keep forever.

225 SDN DZ9F
326 SDN DZ9G

Name	(PLEASE PRINT)	
Address	Apt.#	
City	State/Prov.	Zip/Postal Code

Not valid to current Silhouette Desire® subscribers.

Want to try two free books from another series?
Call 1-800-873-8635 or visit www.morefreebooks.com.

* Terms and prices subject to change without notice. Sales tax applicable in N.Y.
** Canadian residents will be charged applicable provincial taxes and GST.
  All orders subject to approval. Offer limited to one per household.
  ® are registered trademarks owned and used by the trademark owner and or its licensee.

DES04R   ©2004 Harlequin Enterprises Limited

HARLEQUIN *Super Romance*

HOME TO LOVELESS COUNTY
Because Texas is where the heart is.

MORE TO TEXAS THAN COWBOYS

by Roz Denny Fox

Greer Bell is returning to Texas for the first time since
she left as a pregnant teenager. She and her daughter
are determined to make a success of their new dude
ranch—and the last thing Greer needs is romance,
even with the handsome Reverend Noah Kelley.

On sale January 2006

Also look for the final book in this miniseries
The Prodigal Texan (#1326) by Lynnette Kent
in February 2006.

Available wherever Harlequin books are sold.

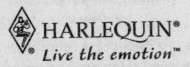

HARLEQUIN®
Live the emotion™

COMING NEXT MONTH

#1699 BILLIONAIRE'S PROPOSITION—Leanne Banks
Battle for the Boardroom
He wants to control a dynasty. She just wants his baby. Who will outmaneuver whom?

#1700 ENGAGEMENT BETWEEN ENEMIES—
Kathie DeNosky
The Illegitimate Heirs
Sometimes the only way to gain the power you desire is to marry your enemy.

#1701 THE MAN MEANS BUSINESS—Annette Broadrick
Business was his only agenda, until his loyal assistant decided to make marriage hers!

#1702 THE SINS OF HIS PAST—Roxanne St. Claire
Did paying for his sins mean leaving the only woman he wanted…for a second time?

#1703 HOUSE CALLS—Michelle Celmer
Doctors do not make the best patients… Here's to seeing if they make the best bedmates….

#1704 THUNDERBOLT OVER TEXAS—Barbara Dunlop
She really wants a priceless piece of jewelry, but will she actually become a cowboy's bride to get it?

SDCNM1205